The Forbidden Stories of Marta Veneranda

The Forbidden Stories
of Marta Veneranda

SONIA RIVERA-VALDÉS

Translated by Dick Cluster, Marina Harss,
Mark Schafer, and Alan West-Dúran

SEVEN STORIES PRESS

New York | London | Toronto | Sydney

Seven Stories Press
140 Watts Street
New York, NY 10013
http://www.sevenstories.com

In Canada:
Hushion House, 36 Northline Road, Toronto, Ontario M4B 3E2

In the U.K.:
Turnaround Publisher Services Ltd., Unit 3, Olympia Trading Estate, Coburg Road, Wood Green, London N22 6TZ

In Australia:
Tower Books, 9/19 Rodborough Road, Frenchs Forest NSW 2086

Library of Congress Cataloging-in-Publication Data

Rivera-Valdés, Sonia.
    [Las historias prohibidas de Marta Veneranda. Spanish]
    The forbidden stories of Marta Veneranda / Sonia Rivera-Valdés.
      p. cm.
    ISBN 1-58322-047-X
I. Title.

PQ7079.2.R55 C8413
863'.64—dc21

                                                00-032936

9 8 7 6 5 4 3 2 1

College professors may order examination copies of Seven Stories Press titles for a free six-month trial period. To order, visit www.sevenstories.com/textbook, or fax on school letterhead to (212) 226-1411.

Printed in the U.S.A.

Contents

Explanatory Note

The stories collected in this volume are true. The names have been changed to protect the identity of the narrators. The idea to collect these confessions over a five-year period grew out of a comment by Professor Arnold Haley. Dr. Haley was speaking in the classroom about a research project, which revealed the disparity between what human beings commonly consider shameful to tell about their lives and the ignominy of the deed itself. That is to say, an individual more often hides a chapter of his or her past because of the way he or she has perceived and experienced it than because of the greater or lesser weight of criminality or social disapproval of the episode itself.

I was in that class and left the room determined to explore this issue. My first question was how many people had, in their past, a story they considered forbidden. I grew obsessed without knowing why. Walking the streets, riding trains, standing in elevators, I studied the expressions on the faces around me and wondered what kind of secrets people carried.

When I spoke with Professor Haley about my project, he

found it interesting not only as a course paper but as a doctoral thesis. Under his supervision, I drew up questionnaires, and began to collect data.

I've always found it easy to relate to people, to establish a certain intimacy with them. As soon as I had interviewed my first subjects, I knew that to understand the complexity of their secrets, I would have to hear about parts of their lives that went far beyond what was covered in the questionnaire. I spoke with Professor Haley who advised that I was missing the concrete details needed to computerize the data I'd obtained, while I had devoted attention to other details that would not allow me to draw any scientifically valid conclusions.

I tried to follow his advice and structure the interviews more systematically. It was an exercise in futility. With each passing day I entered more passionately into the labyrinths of these souls who told me their troubles and torments, and I began to examine mine, to remember events in my own life that I had stubbornly tried to forget.

Dr. Haley insisted on the need for scientific rigor. Unfortunately, against my will and my best interests, our professional differences increased. At my age I shouldn't have been letting disputes like this delay my doctorate. Nonetheless after each recording session, what the transcription consistently offered me was not a set of quantifiable data but a new story too fascinating to resist.

The situation grew more distressing and unbearable until the day a revelation hit me: The solution was not to change my research method but to change my discipline. Though it didn't seem so at first sight, this decision reflected, to a large extent, my devotion to the truth.

The stories published in this volume, selected from among the one hundred seventy-eight I collected, have been chosen so to represent a variety of human conflicts.

—Marta Veneranda Castillo Ovando, Ph.D.

Five Windows on the Same Side

My name is Mayté. Mayté Perdomo. Actually Perdomo Lavalle. That's how I'm registered in Caibarién and how my name appears on my American passport. I hyphenate my two last names to avoid confusion in this country, but sometimes people get mixed up anyway. I'm a journalist. So many lurid things take place in New York every day that hardly anything seems forbidden. But *forbidden* is a relative term. Any event that is embarrassing enough for someone to keep it secret is that person's forbidden story.

You'll judge my story according to your own criteria, but for me this whole matter is very disturbing. Not just that I had a sexual relationship with a woman, but the series of circumstances that surrounded the episode and the impact it had on me. It changed my life.

What have my religious upbringing and education come to, I constantly ask myself. Because no matter how much one has adapted to this society—let's not mince words—among us, homosexuality is not normal. It's not that I'm homophobic. On the contrary. In my work I've defended the rights of gay peo-

ple every time a problem has come up for them, but now, expe-
riencing it in the flesh, it turns out to be more problematic than
I would have thought, had I ever imagined that something like
this could happen to me. I never did, and furthermore it
wouldn't have been so unsettling if it had just been sex. The
flesh is weak, as the nuns at the school in Caibarién used to say,
and anyone can come undone one day.

The worst of it was… I'm embarrassed even to say it… that
I fell in love with her. That's right.

You didn't hear me? I wasn't aware that I had lowered my
voice. I'm sorry. I was saying to you that I fell in love with her.
That frightened me all right. Can you imagine, me wooing
another woman, dancing boleros in a dimly lit room, and buying her flowers? When Alberto found out, he practically died,
the poor thing. He said that one day I was going to give him a
heart attack.

Yes, I told him. We have always been very frank with each
other and I couldn't keep quiet. As soon as he got back from
Chicago, the whole story popped out. Minus the details of
course. It all happened so quickly that my concern might seem
silly, but I've spent whole weekends unable to focus on anything but my obsession about whether I may have been a les-
bian my whole life and not realized it until now. The idea has
screwed me up to the point where I don't even want to see my
little girl, even though she is one of the greatest pleasures in
my life.

The girl is the daughter of Rodolfo, a friend who's like a
brother to me and is also one of my colleagues at the newspaper. He's the only person who knows this story. I haven't even
told Iris, his wife, despite the fact that we're very good friends.
In fact I spend even more time with her than I do with Rodolfo.
We go out together almost every weekend. We take Raquelita,
who is my goddaughter, we stop for lunch somewhere, and we
spend hours walking around this place or that or we go to the
movies. We're both crazy about sales and the knickknacks in
Chinatown, and we've never been able to get either her hus-

band or mine to come with us. I really enjoy these outings. Sometimes I go even though I don't have the time, just to be close to the girl. I want her to remember when she grows up that her godmother was genuinely concerned about her. If I hadn't intended to look after her, I wouldn't have baptized her, and since I don't have children, I adore that sweet little girl. She turned seven in November.

Rodolfo and I share something special. It's not just that he's Cuban, it's that we arrived in New York under the same circumstances, both of us almost the same age. I was thirteen, he was fourteen, and we both came without our parents and went through things that were so painful I don't care to remember. Since then we've tried to joke about them, but our laughter rings hollow. Deep down these experiences are painful and will always be. My mamá says I hold grudges, but no matter how hard I've tried to accept it, I still find it hard to comprehend how a mother could bundle up a thirteen-year-old child, as pampered as she could possibly be by her parents and grandparents, and send her to a foreign country where they don't even speak the same language, without a single relative awaiting her.

Years ago, when Iris, Rodolfo, my husband, and I would go out to eat, as soon as we had a few drinks, Rodolfo and I would start to remember the jams we'd get into in the foster homes where we ended up shortly after arriving in this country when we didn't understand a word of English or how those families worked. In fact it was in one of those houses that we met. And there at the bar the humor would fade right out of the story as we told it and we would end up sobbing, his wife and my husband mortified with embarrassment over the fools we were making of ourselves. We placed the topic off-limits when they were around. They have enough on their hands, being Puerto Rican, without having to deal with our stuff. The truth is that even when they're not around, Rodolfo and I try not to talk about those things, but sometimes they slip out and we always end up feeling that same sadness.

I've been talking for half an hour now and I still haven't started to tell you my story with Laura. I think that your being Cuban makes me remember things I'd thought were forgotten. Let's see how I can organize my thoughts to sum things up.

I tell you, the human mind is fascinating. Just this second, I realized something so obvious it seems incredible that I hadn't thought of it before. Such agony over the episode with Laura, to the point of blaming it for having changed my life, when in reality my confusion began before she appeared. Am I blind for not having seen that?

It all began when Alberto told me that the company where he worked was moving to Chicago and had made him an excellent offer to move there too. Obviously things started with that news. I felt my head spin. It was very strange. A chill ran down my spine all the way to my feet, and then it began running up my body again from my big toe. Only once before in my life had I felt anything like that, and the impression it made on me remained forever.

One night in Cuba. The same thing happened. But that time was even worse. I heard a voice whispering my name so close I felt the heat of the breath on my face. When I turned around, believe it or not, no one was there. It was the night after the telegram authorizing my departure for the United States arrived. My mamá was in the room packing my bag and I had gone onto the porch for a moment. The voice seemed to come from where the jasmine bushes grew. The very same chills ran up and down my body as when Alberto came home with news of the move.

He was so pleased with his raise and the prospect of a new life. It didn't make me happy at all. On the contrary, the idea of leaving New York panicked me, truly panicked me—it's one of those sensations you don't understand until you've experienced it. I couldn't stand the idea of leaving the apartment where I'd lived for so many years. I've lived here since long before I met Alberto. I rented it with the money I earned from my first job.

How could I leave the floorboards where the four legs of my desk stand or my habit of drinking my morning coffee seated on my bed, watching through the window as my neighbors get up? How could I leave the little corner where I meditate, or the space where my computer sits? If I go away, who will guarantee that I'll find again that silent companionship, so special, which I have living among the elderly and people whose constant nighttime activities require that they rest during the day? The point is not to live in the suburbs without anyone nearby, as Alberto said we would live in Chicago, but rather, to be surrounded by people who don't make a racket. How could I leave my walks through the neighborhood, my neighbor who, without even knowing me, would display his meticulous bachelor's life in plain view of my windows, unaware of my interest in him? This is where, for so many years it seems like forever, I have daydreamed of all the good things I wish would happen to me and dreamed at night of houses with many rooms and airplanes that take off without me aboard. I have that dream a lot. And this is where I have felt joy for the good things that have happened and sadness for the bad. And my job—how could he think that I would resign from a job I like so much?

All of that came out of my mouth in a single breath, before I could think.

Obviously he didn't anticipate my reaction and took it as a rejection of his success in the company. He didn't speak to me for a week. That had never happened before. Later, when he'd calmed down, he tried to convince me. Being such a good journalist, I wouldn't have a hard time finding a new job. There are a lot of Latinos in Chicago. I wouldn't have to worry about money if I didn't find a job right away, the two of us could easily live on his salary. It wasn't the end of the world. I would get used to it.

He didn't understand how I could be attached to such a small place in such a difficult and dirty neighborhood when we had a good house on the outskirts of Chicago waiting for us. It

was his dream: land for gardening, a patio for summer barbe-
cues, enough room to have a dog. I knew he had longed for
those things since he was a little boy and it made sense. Anyone
who'd grown up in the confines of a sixth-floor apartment in
the Bronx with four brothers and sisters would have wanted to
live in the country for the rest of their life. But since the possibility of transforming those dreams into reality had never presented itself, I didn't realize that he took them so seriously. In
part, I think his being so tight-lipped—he hardly says a word—
was to blame for the misunderstanding. I told him that, too. I,
on the other hand, being the extroverted person that I am, am
always praising my daily routine, saying how much I love it.
He said he thought I was praising it in an attempt to convince
myself, because we had no alternative to living where we did.
But he never imagined that my celebration was heartfelt. Can
you imagine how out of tune we were with each other for years
without even knowing we were out of tune?

For over ten years Alberto and I seemed to share so many
things in common, and in the end our compatibility was based
on the absence of circumstances to bring out our differences.
That was all. Deep down, he couldn't stand the things that
made up our day-to-day life and that are practically second
nature to me: our apartment, Gladys and her daily phone calls
to tell me the problems she's having with her children, Luisa
and her everlasting spat with Atilio, Esperanza and her loneliness, the homeless, the lines at the corner movie theater, the
Korean fruit stand open twenty-four hours a day. Rodolfo.
How could I go away from Rodolfo and his family? I'd even
miss the prostitutes if I left. My block has been home to prostitutes for over eighty years.

It's not a bad spot. In fact, where I live I'm surrounded by
NYU buildings. It just so happens that once there was a brothel
nearby, on Third Avenue. They shut it down years ago, but the
men still have the habit of picking up women where their
fathers and grandfathers used to do. You know how strong

family traditions are. You may not believe it, but my observation of this phenomenon has helped me to better understand the universality of human behavior. I wrote an article on this topic for the newspaper and people liked it even though it was controversial. They always say that we Latinos are more attached to our families than Americans, but I assure you that the majority of the guys who cruise my block and pick up prostitutes in their car do so because they learned it in the bosom of their family, and the vast majority of them are Americans. Many of them are from New Jersey. I can tell from their license plates.

Luckily I get to watch the spectacle only as I enter and leave my house. I don't think I could stand to see so much human misery all day long. They look so unhealthy that when there's a new face around, the way I find out whether she's a prostitute or not—because you never know—is that I watch her out of the corner of my eye to see the physical shape she's in. If she appears healthy, then I think she isn't one. They often start work at seven in the morning, some of the time practically in the buff, their tits hanging out though it's only twenty degrees. I've watched them waste away by the day, starting out walking the block all plump and after a few months they're nothing but skin and bones. I watched one woman coughing and spitting on the sidewalk for a year while she held back her very long hair with one hand in order not to spit on it. With the other hand, she'd be waving down customers the way you'd wave down a cab. One day she disappeared. She must be dead.

I don't know what got me talking about the prostitutes, with how late it's getting and all. It's my journalistic spirit. In any case, I'm lucky because my apartment overlooks a patio that sits between my building and the one facing it, and I have five windows, all on the same side, which the sun shines through in the afternoon. They face the back of the building. I sleep next to the window in the bedroom and hardly ever raise the blinds. That's the reason I was so mortified the night of the episode with Laura.

She's a second cousin of mine from Cuba I'd never met. She was born two months after I'd left. She's thirty-six years old now, nine years younger than I am, and has two children, a girl of fifteen and a seven-year-old boy. She lived near where I grew up, and her husband, a veteran of the war in Angola, is the father of the boy. The girl's father went to do his doctorate in Russia while they were married, and came back hitched up with a Ukrainian woman. When my cousin found out, he had already had two children with the Russian. They went on for a while longer in that hullabaloo, but finally they got divorced. She was here this time visiting Aunt Rosario, who is quite old and got it into her head that she was going to die without seeing her favorite granddaughter. She made the arrangements all by herself and sent Laura the ticket for the flight to Miami. When I found out that Laura was in the United States, I was so happy, I could have burst. I called her right away and sent her money so that she could come spend a week with me.

She stayed here for two weeks while Alberto was in Chicago. A month after the announcement was made that the company was moving, he had to travel there for business. I was relieved to take a break for a few days from his repeating that I should go with him.

It was in October of last year, sixteen months ago. She arrived in the morning, the day after Alberto left. I went to pick her up at the airport and brought her one of my jackets because it was starting to get cold and she didn't have a coat. Her hair was straight and dark, and she had dimples when she laughed, wide hips like all the women on my mother's side of the family, and tiny feet. That caught my eye. I identified her by sight immediately without us ever having seen each other. She had the very same expression as her mother, my cousin Águeda. We hugged each other tightly and we cried. I don't know why she was crying, but I can say that for me, our meeting meant that standing before me was more than just a relative I was seeing for the first time, but someone with my blood in her veins whose eyes had watched the sun rise and set every day over

Caibarién. Someone who had heard the Cuban birds singing when she woke up, who had stepped on Cuban grass when she went out into the yard. I looked at her, unable to think of anything else, and I cried.

In the taxi we went on like two madwomen, me asking her questions and her telling me all about the family. When we got to my house, I asked her what she wanted to do. I had several plans in mind. "Relax, have some coffee, and talk with you. I want to get to know you," she said. It was Saturday, just like today. It made me happy to think that I had two days to spend with her, and I thanked God for my husband's absence.

Around eight at night I ordered in Chinese food. We weren't hungry, but we nibbled on a few things. After we ate, first Laura took a shower, then I did. I lent her a pink bathrobe, an anniversary present from Alberto. I felt emotionally wiped out, drained. She continued talking. The stories and nostalgia were more than I could take. I offered her a beer, and, in order to stop her talking and to get some rest more than anything else, suggested that we listen to a record of boleros by Marta Valdés, which she'd brought me as a gift. She liked the idea. I didn't know who Marta Valdés was, but I didn't say so. In fact, until that night I'd hardly ever listened to that kind of Cuban music. A little salsa, the Vanván, Pablo Milanés, Silvio Rodríguez, sure, but not boleros. That was my mother's music.

I sat at one end of the sofa. Laura lay down and without asking permission rested her head on my lap, as naturally as can be. It bothered me a bit, but it occurred to me that people in Cuba have more physical contact in their day-to-day life than we do here. I leaned back against the sofa to enjoy the moment. Immersed in my memories more than listening to the music, I began to caress her damp, flowing hair. After a few minutes the melodies had transported me to the straight, narrow streets always ending at the sea, where I used to run as a child. I started to feel the gentle touch of those afternoons, and something inside me began to soften up.

I wasn't paying attention to the song lyrics. My eyes closed,

I was thinking of Caibarién. Suddenly, without meaning to, I listened to the words: *I knew you were coming, though you I didn't know the day. The birds from all the forest told me you were on your way.*

I realized what I was doing with my hand and pulled it from Laura's hair so abruptly that she sat up and asked what was wrong. "Nothing," I answered, but I was feeling uncomfortable. Maybe it's just my imagination, I thought to myself. And yet her head weighed on my thighs as if she were intentionally pressing against them. I wanted to go to my room, to run away. I leaned back against the sofa again, hiding my confusion. The record would be over soon and this bad spell would then pass.

The music ended and instead of getting up, opening the bed for Laura in the living room, and then going to my own bedroom, I did something I never would have expected from myself: I asked her if she had ever heard Lucesita Benítez. She said she had. And I—me!—went over and put on the most romantic record on the face of the earth. No sooner had Lucesita begun then I started, realizing what I had done. What do I do now? My alarm was growing by the second. Laura, in contrast, seemed at ease. Sitting by my side, she was humming along with the song. More than anything else, I felt ridiculous, out of control—the thing I hate most in the world. She slowly slid down and lay her head on my lap again, my legs now rigid. My efforts to appear unruffled made every muscle in my body contract. I was nearly trembling. *Two days without your love, two days without your touch. Our time is so precious, and we've wasted so much,* went the bolero. Do you know it, Marta Veneranda? It's absolutely lovely.

"I love this bolero," Laura said enthusiastically. "It's been ages since I've heard it. Would you like to dance?"

We danced. Very close. I had never danced like that with a woman, our cheeks grazing one another. It was very soft. As the bolero played, we danced more and more slowly, closer and closer.

Can't you see that I'm yours, that you own my heart, that nothing on earth can drive us apart?

Without letting go of me, she pulled her face away from mine and looked me straight in the eyes. She just looked at me without blinking, that's all. I don't know how to explain it. My legs grew weak like when I feel like going to bed with a man, but there was something different this time: weakness mixed with strength, a yearning to conquer her, to possess her. That's what I felt.

I held her around the waist, drawing her toward me with a strength I didn't recognize. I felt wet and sensed that she was too. The idea of her body feeling the same as mine was driving me wild.

By the time the record was over, we had been kissing for the last three songs, our hips swaying in time to the music. The softness of her neck, her arms, her back delighted me. Such a different sensation from that of embracing a man. I couldn't stop thinking of that.

I took her hand and led her to my bed. I took her. I didn't even bother to take off the floral bedspread I am so careful with because I love it. After Laura left, I took it to the dry cleaners, but it's never been the same. I still put it on the bed because of the memories it evokes.

I caressed and kissed every piece and fold of that body with an intensity and passion I had never put into my lovemaking before, and she reciprocated with furious splendor. We spent hour after hour fused to one another. Sated at last, exhausted, we lay on our backs pushing aside the panties and brassieres strewn across the flowers of the bedspread. The light of the lamp on the night table illuminated our bodies. Neither of us had remembered to turn it off.

I closed my eyes for a few minutes. When I opened them, Laura was sleeping where she lay. That's when I realized that I hadn't lowered the blind over the window and the bed was right in view. The neighbor in the apartment facing mine, the bachelor, watched indifferently, standing at his kitchen sink.

As I sat up, he began to wash lettuce for a salad for his late nightly dinner. He does it every night. Obviously he had seen. I lowered the blind and didn't raise it again for the two weeks Laura spent here, most of which we spent in bed and dancing boleros in the living room. I even called in sick to work for three days.

We got out so little that when she left I felt guilty for not having shown her more of New York. But I console myself by thinking that the few outings we did take were due to my insistence. If it had been up to her, we wouldn't have left the radius of my apartment and the restaurants around it. At least I took her to Chinatown, Rockefeller Center, Saint Patrick's Cathedral, Harlem; we saw the Lower East Side and took a trip on the Circle Line. That was fantastic, a brilliant idea. I will remember it a thousand years from now. I have never felt so romantic in my whole life, except in the movies, especially watching *From Here to Eternity*. Except that while watching the movie I was sure that I was Deborah Kerr, whereas on the Circle Line, in all honesty, I could never figure out if I was her or Burt Lancaster.

I was aghast at my own behavior, but Laura seemed at ease. She admitted that this wasn't the first time this had happened, although with me it was something special. I didn't believe the second part. I asked if her husband knew.

"Are you nuts? How would he know?" she responded, looking at me as if I were kidding.

"I'm going to tell Alberto," I said. "Otherwise, I couldn't live in peace with myself."

Her eyes widened. She was flabbergasted.

"You're crazy in the head," she said, shaking her own from side to side. "Look. My first husband was with the Ukrainian woman for years before I found out. She even bore him a pair of twins behind my back. César, my current man, is very good, but do you think I don't know that he sleeps with any woman that comes along as soon as he has the chance? I'm not going to pass up a good time myself when it appears. I have no interest in affairs with men. I look to women for that. What can you do? To each her own, and besides, there's no risk of getting pregnant."

We sat down to talk several times, don't think we didn't. But we were speaking different languages whenever we spoke of this matter. In the final analysis, now that I've calmed down, I think this was the most astonishing part of the experience— the different weight we gave to things. Laura didn't understand how I, with the worldliness she attributed to me because of my education, the trips I've taken, the exposure I've had to different cultures, my living in such a cosmopolitan city, could think that not to tell Alberto what had happened would be an act of betrayal. There are things one doesn't tell was her motto. She didn't understand my idea of honesty. The fact that this was the only way I could live in peace with myself seemed to her to be a sign of immaturity. To her mind my confession would, in the best of cases, cause needless suffering for Alberto and in the worst, cause a tragedy for us both. "What you don't know won't hurt you." In short, she was my cousin; it was perfectly normal that she would have stayed with me. Why complicate matters? She didn't live here. God only knew when we would see each other again.

"You think I'm going to go back to Cuba and tell César about this? What for?"

We parted without my understanding her need to live a secret life nor her understanding my need to lead an open one.

I write to her now and then, whenever I find someone who is going to Cuba, and Laura does the same when a friend is coming this way. You know how difficult communication with the island is. Family letters, as if nothing had ever happened. Mine are more laconic, but she writes page after page talking about the children and the aunts and cousins we have in common. A short while ago she asked me for a hair straightener for a friend of hers. Before that she had asked for lipstick and some creams for the same girl. They're neighbors and apparently they get along well. I bought her the straightener and I'll send it to her as soon as I can.

Laura left for Miami the same day Alberto returned from Chicago. I took her to the airport in the morning and he arrived at six thirty in the evening. Between her departure and his arrival I considered the effects of what had happened. There was no question: I was not about to move to Chicago now. Alberto wouldn't keep asking because he wouldn't want me to go with him. This thought relieved me.

We had dinner that night at a Thai restaurant. I thought I would talk to him the next day, after he had rested, but as soon as he went into the bedroom he asked why the blind was down. I only pull it down when I make love with him. I looked at him, looked at the blind, and I swear I tried to make up some excuse so that I could go to sleep early, I was so tired. But as always happens with me, the whole story popped out of my mouth before I could stop it. When I finished, he said:

"All right. Now you're going to have to go to Chicago with me. You can't live with the blinds pulled and you won't dare raise them." I wondered how much he loved or needed me. Who knows.

It was difficult, but he realized that after what had happened, I needed to be by myself for a while. It had all been so surprising, the discovery of a loose end in me that I had to tie up somehow. It was no longer New York or the apartment; it was something more serious.

He moved a year ago. I'm still in my little apartment with my furniture, my favorite nooks, my neighbors, my street, my friends, my work, Raquelita on the weekends, and my blinds open.

After I finished talking with Alberto, very late that night, I went to bed. The next morning I made coffee while he was still asleep and slowly raised the blind. Would you believe that my neighbor's apartment was empty? The first thing I noticed when I started to roll up the blind was that the canary yellow sofa where my neighbor would spend hours upon hours reading on his days off was gone. I'm sure that he taught in a university and used to prepare his classes lying there.

They painted the apartment white, sanded the floor, and a few days later two men came to live there. They put a black sofa with light purple roses on it in the living room. They cook more often than the previous neighbor and don't eat dinner as late.

I've bought more bolero records. I have a huge collection. That was one of the positive effects of Laura's visit. In general I'm doing well. I would even go so far as to say that I'm happy to have discovered a new angle on my life. Good journalist that I am, curiosity is one of my outstanding characteristics.

To be honest, what disturbs me at this point, after having this conversation with you, during which I've clarified several things for myself—the magical power of language—is not knowing, despite the explanations I gave Alberto, whether I didn't go to Chicago because of the problem with Laura, or whether the problem with Laura was caused by my desire to find a reason not to go to Chicago.

The Scent of Wild Desire

I don't know where to start. I'm afraid of telling it and having you think I'm crazy—or worse, that I'm a pig—but if I don't tell somebody, I'll end up truly beyond the beyond, and maybe I'll find it easier with you, ma'am, precisely because I don't know you and I'll probably never see you again. And besides, if, as Mayté says, you've spent more than two years hearing people tell you things they haven't dared to say to another soul, well, maybe my story won't seem so weird, because God knows what else you've heard. Mayté's own story is pretty crazy, in truth. But mine is worse. I swear it.

This story is so strange and different from what my life has been like up till now that nobody's going to recognize me in it. That it should have happened to me is truly strange, because I'm so committed to cleanliness that I'll take a bath even if I'm running a fever of a hundred and four. You're Cuban; you know the fixation we Cubans have about smells. For us, stinking is a capital crime. Who among all who know me is going to think I did what I did? Nobody. Not even my wife would believe it, and I've lived with her for more than ten years.

I'm going to tell you the whole truth. I came here because Mayté insisted so much, and I feel so... I don't know... let's say... disconcerted, disturbed, messed up, who knows. The thing is that because I can't manage to forget this shit—and pardon the bad language—she told me that I had to at least give you a try. Maybe this conversation can somehow get it all off my mind, like what happened to her with all that about Laura, because according to what she says, telling it relieved her like magic, and I know pretty well how heavily that thing was weighing on her. But let me tell you, my first reaction when she suggested this was to reject it one hundred percent. How could she think that I was going to tell somebody I didn't even know about something that I can't spit out even to the people closest to me, such as Mayté herself? You can imagine how I feel. Look at me, sitting here talking to you. I've told Mayté things I never told Miguel, who's been my friend since we were little; we went to the beach together every day, back in Jaimanitas. Miguel, who, thanks to life's twists and turns, is now here, living in New York.

But what brought me to see you, not for the life of me am I going to tell it to either of them. What happened is that Mayté knows me too well, we've been working together for years at the paper, and she saw right away that something was eating at me, though at first I denied it and told her that I was just tired, that nothing was going on. Imagine, me, with my reputation for writing with ease, I've been waiting till the last minute to crank out my articles, and writing them badly too. It takes such an effort for me to concentrate, and even to speak coherently. Look at this conversation I'm having with you, that hasn't got any beginning or end. Normally I'm an articulate individual, and well mannered too.

Sure, I know a therapist. I not only know one, I've been going to one for a long time. I know I could go see him, I've thought about it a lot, but no way, I'm not telling this to him. I'd die first, from the shame of him knowing about this. After all these years we're friends, don't you see? He'll think I've gone crazy if he hears this string of nutty things. Believe me. He's known me since I was fifteen, fresh from Cuba. It was because of an obsession I was having about the beach at Jaimanitas, where I lived until I was fourteen.

Yes, that's how it was, with Operation Peter Pan. That operation screwed up so many people.

In fact, no, my mother didn't get so hysterical. It was my father who was terrified. I've never understood how come, because the old man is no dummy, but it was like his brain turned to mush. He swallowed that whole story about how the state was going to take custody of all the kids away from their parents. Plus I was about to turn fifteen, so I had military service pending, and forget getting me out of Cuba after that. So the first chance that came along, he packed me off without giving it a second thought. My mother cried and pleaded that I shouldn't be sent out of the country alone.

They came here a year later. Did I have a hard time? Real hard. I lived with three different families. None of them could stand me, and I couldn't stand them. You know how spoiled Cuban children are, and to be dropped as if by parachute into a strange country, such a different culture, a new language! I don't want to remember. But the thing was that while I was alone, I didn't think about anyone but them, and then, as soon as they got here and I had a more or less normal family again, I started to miss this girlfriend I'd left behind at the beach. A lovely girl. I liked her, you can't imagine how much. And I got to thinking, but I mean thinking day and night, that was the problem, that every afternoon she was going with another guy to the same bridge where we two used to go to watch the sun set, the last few months that I lived there.

Now it seems incredible that I could have suffered so much for such a silly thing, but at that point I practically gave up eating for days at a time and went whole nights without shutting my eyes.

It was a bridge by the sea, over a narrow canal. Wooden, small, and half ruined by the waves that pounded it when the sea was choppy. Hardly anybody used it and the bottom was full of shellfish. It wasn't even a good place for romancing; the little bridge was close to the pier where the fishermen tied their boats in the early morning after a night of fishing, and where they cleaned their fish. But I was a boy, and for me those afternoons were the most beautiful in the world, leaning against the rail of the bridge with my girl, one arm around her waist and trying to get the other hand down her blouse. They were glorious, ma'am, glorious.

The psychologist helped me out a lot and finally I got over my depression. I kept on seeing him, because I realized that the problems inside my head had to do with more than that girlfriend. Now it's been a while since I've seen him, and he thinks I'm in as good shape as can be. And really, I was, until this happened. No way… I'm not going to tell him. Look, I've been all over it in my mind, over and over, and I can't find any explanation. Two months now and I still think about it when I get up and think about it when I go to bed. It's much worse than that business about Jaimanitas. Much worse.

Yes, I know I'm going around in more circles than a spinning top, of course I know that. But it's such an effort to get started.

It was a Saturday morning. Iris had left early to see her mother in New Jersey and wasn't going to be back until late. She took the girl with her. Around ten I was getting ready to sit down and read, happy about the idea of a few hours' peace and quiet, when somebody knocked on the door. It seemed strange because almost no one knocks on the apartment door without us having to open the downstairs lobby door first. I looked through the peephole, and before I could see who it was, I heard a woman's voice saying that something terrible had happened. It was the neighbor from the apartment next door. I opened up, and she said all in a rush that it was an emergency. She'd been straightening up the house for its weekend cleaning and filling the bathtub for her bath. She went out in the corridor with a ton of old newspapers to put them next

to her door so that she could take them down to the recycling
bin in the basement later on, when, suddenly, the door closed
and locked behind her. Nobody in the building had an extra
key to her apartment. A friend across the street used to have
one, but he'd moved not long before, and the super lives out
on Long Island. And to top it off, she'd been about to get into
the bath at the moment when her door shut, so when she
knocked on my door, she was wasn't wearing anything but a
T-shirt which barely reached to the tops of her enormous
thighs—because my neighbor weighs about four hundred
pounds. No, I'm not exaggerating, she's that immensely fat.
My only dealings with her had been mutual greetings when
we met in the hallways or elevators, but often enough Iris and
I had watched through the peephole of our door her morning
trip from the apartment to the elevator; her weight astonished
us, and the curious way she walked, swaying from one side to
the other.

I asked her to come in. She entered swaying, and the thin
cloth of the T-shirt let me see the heaping balls of fat that hung
under her arms, around her hips, from her thighs. Her chest-
nut hair was loose and her light gray eyes looked almost
transparent. I'd never seen her so close up. A very pretty face,
smooth skin, slightly thick lips, and straight white teeth. I went
to the kitchen to rummage in a drawer for the emergency
phone number, to get ahold of someone from the building's
maintenance department who would take care of the situation.
If we couldn't contact anyone, then we'd call a locksmith.

That's when the part that's hard to tell started. When I
closed the door behind her and she started toward the living
room couch, a horrible, fetid odor burst into the apartment. I
won't try to describe it, because I've tried, mentally, all this
time, and I haven't been able to. Very strong. The strongest I've
ever smelled in my life. A little sour and kind of salty, maybe
like shellfish rotting along the edge of a beach after they've
been in the sun for several days. At first I only smelled it, with-

out thinking, but as the stench grew the farther in she came, I thought it must have been in my head. It couldn't come from my neighbor, a woman with a normal apartment, a job, with friends who came to visit her. But when she sat down and I got close to give her the phone book so that she could find a locksmith—since the super turned out to be impossible to reach—I was convinced that in fact she was giving off a fearful stink. She hadn't bathed in at least a week. I was nauseous, I swear, that's how strong the smell was. The whole situation seemed unreal, as if I were watching a movie or something. She finished her phone call and reported that the locksmith was busy with another emergency at the moment, but he'd be there in half an hour to help out. Half an hour, I thought. I didn't know if I could stand it. I didn't want to be inhospitable, though.

I sat down across from her in an armchair, instead of next to her on the couch, while I tried to pretend that my nose didn't exist and to ignore the heaves that would rise up from my stomach to my throat every time I forgot to forget the stench.

We started to talk about how wrong it was not to have a superintendent living in the building, and from that we moved on to commenting how lucky it was that all the neighbors on the sixth floor got along so well. The stink emanating from that woman invaded the room. She was leaning back against the back of the couch now, with her legs half open; they were impossible to close because of the diameter of her thighs. At first I tried not to breathe with normal regularity, but caught between suffocating myself or inhaling the rotten sea creatures I felt myself submerged among, well, I decided to breathe. I listened to the rhythm and intonation of the sound that came out of her mouth, without paying attention to the words. By the time ten minutes had gone by I couldn't hear anymore. All my energy was dedicated to getting through this ordeal.

All of a sudden her expression grew more meaningful. It didn't match the triviality of the conversation anymore. Her big gray eyes, locked on mine, didn't blink. Her eyes and mouth sent me different messages. She kept on talking in a low, warm tone—because she had a lovely voice, too.

Then the weirdest thing in the world happened. All of a sudden I realized I was breathing as hard as I could. I don't mean normally, but with all my lungs, like in a yoga exercise. The stench was gone, transformed into a deep aroma that I was eager to breathe in. Leaning back languidly on the couch, her thighs more open now, the woman was displaying her dark sex that gave off that intoxicating odor, because that was where the powerful fragrance was welling from. And I didn't think anymore. I don't know which of my faculties quit functioning, but all of a sudden we stopped talking and I was staring openly at her shadowy cave and breathing in that odor, breathing deep. I wanted to sink into it, wanted it to envelop and devour me. With effort she shifted position a few times, then spread her legs completely and the folds of her open vulva exhaled a perfume that now entranced me. I went wild. She fell back on the sofa and pulled up the T-shirt with her hands, exposing her gigantic breasts and the three hundred pounds of flesh that surrounded them. I went nuts, I swear that I went nuts. Wild. Nothing like this had ever happened to me. The only sane thing I managed to do, thank God, was to get a condom out of the desk drawer where I always keep a few in case Iris and I get a sudden notion while we're watching television after the girl is asleep, and I put it on. There wasn't any romance. And listen, I'm a romantic type, even in the most difficult of situations: I told you the story about Jaimanitas. But this was a whole other thing. I went to her with my pants down, before I could finish taking them off. I climbed on top of her and penetrated her — slowly at first, but then strong and savage. She let it happen. She took me soft and open, and so big there on the couch that she couldn't fit and her flesh hung off the edge and, in the middle of all that I was trying to grab hold so that she wouldn't fall on the floor. I sank into her body. That fragrance was all around me, and the more I smelled, the more I wanted to smell. My nose explored her whole body, searching out the most hidden places, the ones with the strongest smell where the accumulated fat created labyrinths of skin. Can you imagine this?

Really, it didn't last ten minutes. When the locksmith called on the intercom, I jumped off the couch. She lowered her T-shirt, I opened the door, and while she was walking to her apartment, she thanked me for the hospitality.

When I went back in my apartment and closed the door, I came to my senses and almost fainted from the nauseating stink. I lit incense and opened the windows even though it was below zero out. The smell abated, but I couldn't read, thinking about what had happened. In the afternoon I made *arroz con pollo* with a lot of garlic and olive oil, to fill the apartment with those odors before Iris got home. But as soon as she came in, she asked what smelled so strange. I said it was probably the mixture of incense and spices. "Maybe," she said, "but it smells like the ocean to me."

The next morning, when we opened the door to get the newspaper, we found three splendid pears and a thank-you note signed by our neighbor. I told Iris how she'd ended up in the hallway with no keys and I'd helped her take care of the problem. Every now and then I run into her and we greet each other with that same impersonal cordiality as we did before she got locked out, but I haven't stopped being mortified by what went on.

Tell me, ma'am, how would you explain the fact that some-body like me, who's never been able to stand the smell of sweat, should enjoy one that's so much worse? How far would I have gone if the locksmith hadn't arrived? That's what worries me the most. In the end, one doesn't know what one is capable of, given certain circumstances. If it weren't for the condom, which I kept and I look at now and then, I'd think it was a nightmare.

Why do I keep it? I don't know. I just don't know.

Between Friends

I f what I'm about to tell you happened, then it's a truly forbidden story, so much so that I'm only going to tell you
because I have complete trust in your discretion. If you
talked about it, I could go to jail, though there's a chance that
my memory is wrong, in which case the sin would only be in
my imagination. I don't know. I have some friends I could ask,
and find out whether the story is true, because they were there.
But I'm never going to do that.

People are strange. It might just be me, but I don't think so.
It happens to everybody. People have told me so many things
without my asking them. There are parts of our past we'd like
to erase, never mention, and suddenly one day we feel the
need to speak and our tongue loosens up. It's a dangerous
temptation; that's why the proverb says the milkman wasn't
killed for watering down the milk but for admitting that he
did. I thought my lips were sealed for all eternity about this
matter, but when Iris, the lawyer I work for, told me two weeks
ago how good her friend Mayté felt after coming to see you, I
got an urge to tell my story. Mayté is that journalist who had a
romance, if you can call it that, with a cousin who came from

Cuba to visit her. Do you remember? I'm not speaking out of turn, she doesn't know I know about it. It's just so you'll understand why I'm here.

My case is different. I haven't come because of feeling bad. On the contrary, I'm doing better than ever before. I've got a good job as an executive secretary, my own little apartment; my son supports himself and has a decent job. What more could I ask? I never dreamed I'd have so much.

Maybe, it occurs to me just this minute, I'd like to have what I've got without paying the price that I paid.

The first time I came to this country was in the late sixties, after a lot of last-minute complications. I was fulfilling a great dream I'd had since I was little, when Uncle Silvester would come visit us in Peru, and I would watch him arrive, weighed down by presents for all of us. It was like a ray of hope: to go to the United States. When I got here, he'd been living in California for about thirty-five years.

I overslept and missed the plane, thanks to the farewell party my friends threw the night before, but I caught the next day's flight, and my friend Monica was waiting for me in Miami. A few days later I went to visit my uncle. He was so happy to see me! I spent a whole month going around San Diego with him and his wife. I was amazed by the variety of people, so different from the ones in my country. In Miami, Cubans. In California, Mexicans. So many different accents I could hear.

Then I decided to go back to Miami, where I started working without papers in some rich people's house. I was there for six months. I didn't earn much and only went out on weekends to visit my Peruvian friend, but I felt safe and protected. Only one thing disturbed my peace of mind. My mother, who like all mothers had this big fear of losing her child, kept sending me word that my boss was calling her every day to find out when I would be coming back to work—it was one of those government jobs you only get if somebody puts in a word for you. At the same time, Immigration here started pestering me with a constant stream of letters. They threatened to deport me if I didn't the country.

The owners of the house were two men who were very happy with me. Percy, the older one, was already seventy but didn't look it. He wasn't a bad guy; he took me out to eat once in a while during the time I was working there, without me ever suspecting his intentions. One morning, after I served them breakfast, they made a proposal. "You're a pretty girl," the younger one said. "I'd marry you and solve your residency problem, but I can't because I'm only separated from my wife. But you can marry my friend Percy; he's a single man with a lot of money. Take a good look at him. He's got blue eyes." Percy turned red, hearing his friend; he was shy. I thought the point of the offer was to provide the old man with a permanent nurse, so I didn't accept. My idea was to marry for love. Luckily I'd saved enough money over those six months to go back to my country and my government job.

My American dream was still going strong, though, and two years later I came back, this time to New York with some neighbors of mine as starry-eyed as me. I didn't like Miami, where Immigration is always breathing down your neck. We thought we'd go to Newark, where Monica had moved, but fate set us down in New York.

When the three of us landed in the airport, scared out of our wits, we decided to grab a taxi. We asked the driver to take us to a not-so-expensive hotel and he took us right to a fleabag in Brooklyn. The man at the front desk, a very friendly Indian from Trinidad, asked us a bunch of questions about who we were. He put us in a room that was pretty tight for three people, but we had space to spare because we were so terrified that all three of us squeezed into one bed. We didn't sleep. All night we watched the door, thinking that any second somebody was going to come barging in.

The next morning the man from Trinidad, who was still at the desk, inquired why we needed to go to Newark and said he could talk with a woman he knew who would rent us a room. In a flash he called her and made the deal. She was a Dominican lady, a mother with a fourteen-year-old girl and three little boys, ages three, two, and one. Those three would all fit under a single basket, as we say in my country. The man from the hotel, who was married to another woman and had other kids, was also Yokasta's lover and the father of the little boys. He came to see her to make more children, that's all. She gave us room and board for very little money, in exchange for us obeying two rules: We couldn't come in after eleven at night or bring men into our room.

That afternoon after we put away our things, they took us for a drive to Rockaway Beach. It was almost the end of August, and we were so happy and hopeful about our new life that not even the suffocating heat bothered us. Everything seemed interesting. We got out of the car and while my friends Anita and Victoria watched a game of handball, which was new to them, I walked down the sand toward the edge of the beach. I went walking along the seashore with my shoes off and my feet in the water. Two men in bathing suits were watching me from where they sat on the sand. One of them came up to me and asked for my name and phone number, the way men do. I didn't speak English. I called Victoria over, who knew some, and she translated. He said his name was Joe and that he'd call me soon.

I waited nervously, but nothing happened over the next few days. My friends and I decided to start taking English classes at night in a public school. We met tons of Italians there. One of them, Nicky, asked me out. He took me to dinner in Manhattan, at a brightly lit restaurant in Little Italy. We went with my two girlfriends and two friends of his. After that we kept going out from time to time.

When I was least expecting it, one Sunday afternoon two weeks after my first date with that classmate, Joe called and invited me out too.

As soon as I opened the door he smiled, bowed his head in a ceremonious way, and held out a bouquet of flowers in his right hand. They were red roses with a white bud in the middle of the bouquet. In his left hand he had a bag with juice, milk, and food. For a while I kept going out with both of these friends. Every Friday for about six months Joe sent me a basket of red roses with a white bud in the center, and then he proposed to me. Nicky was sad, but he left the scene. I wrote to my parents in Peru about my engagement and they happily agreed.

Joe had round cheeks and gray eyes that were maybe too hard, but I was fascinated by him, and especially by the suffering he'd gone through in Poland. The terrible story of him and his family during World War II was so different from anything I'd known in my life. He'd gone through a lot, even eating rats. He had a lot of different skills and a great talent for music. He played accordion and piano and sang in public. He liked the beach, fishing, and picnicking. He gave parties, invited people over for drinks, and spent all his money on them. Though he earned plenty, once we were married, I never knew where his wages went. He was a karate expert and could handle guns like a professional because he'd been trained in the "organization." That was a secret he couldn't discuss with anyone. The "organization" had recruited him while he was still in Poland because he spoke more than six languages, and they helped him get out of there. Right after he got to the U.S., they sent him to various South American countries. To me he was a James Bond. How could I not go crazy over that kind of man? I'd never known anybody like him, outside of movies. Cultured, good-looking, with good qualities.

On December 24th, Christmas Eve, he brought me a diamond ring and said he wanted to give it to me at Midnight Mass in a church on Long Island near where his mother and sister lived. They'd be coming to the mass to meet me for the first time. He proposed we spend the night at his family's house. I told him I had to be back at my landlady Yokasta's house by eleven. That was her rule, and I'd always respected it. There was no way I could stay out all night. It would be unacceptable to her. He kept insisting, but I didn't give in. Suddenly he flew into a rage like I'd never seen before and said that if I wasn't going to sleep with him, he wouldn't give me the diamond ring. He took it with him and I never saw it again. Later I found out he'd buried it that night at the same beach where we'd met, near some rocks. The next morning I went looking for it but couldn't find it. I spent a long time searching on my hands and knees, digging in the sand. After a few hours my back was sunburned, but the ring never appeared.

His sister helped us plan the wedding, but they had a fight before the wedding day and ended up not speaking. She claimed it was because of his binges, but at that point I'd never seen him drink except in social gatherings. Sometimes he drank a lot, but always at parties, and nothing unpleasant would ever happen.

We got married all by ourselves, on the outs with everyone, fighting with them like cats and dogs. After the argument with his sister the parties stopped, and he wouldn't even invite my girlfriends or Yokasta to the wedding. He said he didn't want to spend anything on anyone. We went to the courthouse on Queens Boulevard to have the ceremony. I put on a short white dress and we had a bottle of champagne, just us two. That was it. Despite that distressing beginning, I went happily to live in his apartment. I was very lonely because my girlfriends, of course, were offended about not being invited to the wedding, so they were giving me the cold shoulder. What a big mistake I'd made!

I got pregnant and had a hard time, lots of vomiting; I couldn't keep anything down for the first four months. Around then Joe started coming home in a weird state. I couldn't really talk with him. When he came home from work, he'd assault me with questions: What had I done, had I gone out, and if so, why? Every night he'd be strange like that and I didn't know what it was about until, without anybody's help or advice, I studied him and figured out all by myself that he was drinking. Even his face changed. Sometimes he confused me with his first wife's lover, a Cuban homosexual who worked as a cutter in Joe's little curtain factory. Joe had been the owner of this business, that is, but he lost it all in the divorce. By the time I met him he was working for someone else.

That's true, I forgot to tell you Joe was married before and had five children with his first wife, including a pair of twins. Apparently he suffered a lot with her. He said he had trusted the Cuban homosexual, whom he thought was his friend and anyway no threat as far anything romantic was concerned. Then one day he came home at an unusual time, saw the friend's car parked outside the building, went up and found it very quiet when he opened the door. He started walking slowly toward the bedroom and found the guy in bed with his wife, doing the same thing he would have done if he hadn't been queer. Joe said that was why he didn't trust women. In the morning he'd leave me with kisses and hugs. At night he'd come home drunk and ask me all the same questions. What had I done, had I gone out, and why? Each time he was louder and more insistent. He was losing so much respect for me that the insulting questions were nothing compared to the other things he did. One night he came home and after the questions he hit me and then he grabbed my dress by the shoulders and lifted me up so quickly and angrily that I had bruises in my armpits for days. I was heavy with the pregnancy by then.

So time went by, the baby was born, and for me things were going from bad to worse. One day outside the apartment door I found a big pile of unlit matches. It struck me as really strange, and when he got home that night I asked him what it was about. Every day, he said, when I closed the door behind him, he stood a match up against the door. So if the door opened the match would fall and when he got back in the afternoon and I told him I hadn't gone out, he'd know I'd lied. Since my son was walking by this time, he'd go play next to the door. He'd bump into it and the match would fall. That confirmed Joe's suspicions even though there wasn't any basis for them.

At night he'd pick up the plate of food I set out for him on the table, throw it against the wall or sink, and then be on me with his fists, yelling for me to clean up the mess. I'd run away before he could hurt me any worse. That was all getting to be a habit. I was always bruised, my mouth swollen, black eyes, my head full of lumps. Every night was a torment. In my vain hope that things would improve, I tried to keep the house impeccably clean, his food hot and ready when he came home, his shorts and undershirts clean and folded, but his pattern was to come in drunk—sometimes more, sometimes less—with crazy accusations and demands. I didn't know where to hide. I told myself I would swallow dirt. I wanted to die. He'd come home and call me over, rudely, "Come sit here next to me," he'd say, which was the beginning of an interrogation about my former boyfriends, especially Nicky. He claimed he had friends who were private detectives and that one of them was darker-skinned, didn't look American, spoke Spanish, and he'd sent this one to spy on me while I was talking with my women friends. He said he'd found out that I kept seeing Nicky after I was already engaged to him. He tortured me, claiming I'd been Nicky's lover and demanding that I had to tell him what we'd done. When I'd say "Nothing!" then wham!—I'd get a smack in the face. "Talk! Where did you go with him!" I'd start to cry and he'd keep on punching me. Sometimes he'd come after me in the bathroom. Once, when I was getting out of the shower, he started to beat me and I fell against the edge of the tub. I hit my forehead and bled all over the place. He threw me a towel that got almost completely soaked. I cried so much during my life with him, I think I could have filled a bucket with my tears. I wouldn't wish that on my worst enemy. Years went by, years when I didn't know what to do. I prayed, suffered, cried, and shivered. I'd put the boy to bed early to save him the terrible sight of his mother being humiliated, and afterward I'd pray to heaven for help. I always made the boy say his prayers before bed and sometimes, when my husband wasn't drunk, we'd all three pray together. He was very Catholic.

At first he didn't let me work because of his jealousy, but when the boy started school, I got a few odd jobs cleaning house for the Jews who lived around us. Later I started to take care of old people who were sick. I got paid better for that. I had a talent for it, the nurses said, and I learned to work the oxygen tanks, change the I.V. bottles when they were empty, and even give emergency shots and insulin shots to diabetics. On paydays Joe would say, "Put the money on the table." We paid all the bills fifty-fifty, and the rest went into his pocket for him to spend. I was as broke as if I hadn't earned a penny, and had to be beg him for money. He only bought me the bare necessities. Whatever else I had came as presents from the women I worked for. I worked more and more, to the point where I was working six days a week for ten years, until after I became a widow.

One those many nights when he came home drunk, he repeatedly confused me with his ex-wife's Cuban lover. He called me by his name, Marcelo, and attacked me with karate kicks. His heel caught me in the face. My blood ran like a river, the whole right side swelled up and forced my eye closed. I started screaming. I didn't care anymore, I screamed as loud as I could. It was about two in the morning. Friday and Saturday nights were always the worst, between ten at night and three in the morning. Still hurling insults, he took me to the emergency room of a little hospital that was closing when we showed up. They didn't even have equipment to take an X ray. He picked up the phone himself, there in the hospital, and called the police. When they came, they asked me did I want to send him to jail. I told them no, because I thought he'd kill me when he got out.

Sometimes he'd wake up in the middle of the night to find himself alone in bed, and then he'd come for me and find me sleeping on the living room sofa, all beaten up. He'd be shocked, surprised, with no memory of doing this to me. He'd ask me to forgive him, but then he'd do it all over again.

At Christmas, after we'd finished setting up the tree, he wanted to knock it down. The boy had spent the whole day decorating it. He ran and stood in front of the tree to protect it. Joe started beating him, savagely, without caring where his fists would hit. He broke open the boy's forehead and the blood poured down over one eye. I got in the way and he turned his fury on me. This all happened often enough. Then the boy and I would lie in bed for hours, holding each other tight, trying to soothe the wounds that we didn't deserve. We lived through horror. Suddenly he'd appear with his they-tell-me-you-did-this and they-tell-me-you-did-that, and he'd smash old photos because he saw a man in them when there wasn't any there.

I didn't put up with so much out of masochism, or because I like getting beaten. It's that I didn't know how I could leave. He threatened me, saying that wherever I went he'd find me and destroy me. I was terrorized, and I couldn't criticize him, because he denied being an alcoholic. He also smoked a lot, more and more. He got up to three packs a day.

As a result of those twelve years of marriage, I've got a cheekbone that's cracked beneath my eye, and one side of my jaw sags to this day. Once, I asked a doctor about that bone and he said, "Don't do anything to it. Leave it alone." I know I have a sunken cheek.

I suffered and suffered, and didn't have a thing, not even residency in this country. I can't find the words to tell you how I felt. More lowly than a cockroach and completely helpless. After more than ten years of marriage, I pleaded with him to buy some land, and he agreed. Perhaps it was because he was starting to feel ill, although even he didn't realize it, and didn't have the fight in him anymore. We went to upstate New York and bought a cottage on a six-acre piece of land, with fruit trees and some hills that the boy and I went sledding down that winter when they were covered with snow. Way up north, near Canada, where they call the Hudson the North River and it's narrower than the river we see down here. The house was a log cabin, tiny, with an old chimney, but I liked going there so much.

When spring came, he was coughing a lot. He didn't have any appetite, only drank alcohol. He didn't want to drive, so the trips to the country got more and more sporadic. The flowers I had planted with such care were dead, which made me so sad. I told him to go to the doctor. At first he ignored me, but he got sicker and one day decided to go. He left in the morning and came home at night with a mask over his nose and mouth. Sitting in the kitchen, he told me he'd just come to say he had tuberculosis and was going to be hospitalized. I cried, I couldn't believe it. In my country I saw many neighbors die of tuberculosis, but here, with all the food there was in my house, I couldn't believe it. My mother had always been afraid of that disease. She fed us well and sent us for X rays once a year. But here, in such an advanced country! Food was the one thing he bought. He had a psychosis because of what he'd gone through in World War II. He said he'd needed to eat out of the garbage, when people were killing each other over a loaf a bread.

When he was hospitalized, the boy and I were left alone. Monica and Yokasta, my old landlady, found out and started visiting me every so often. The two of them got to be friends. It was so good to recover friendships, to talk again. I had almost forgotten how it felt to have a normal conversation, to share opinions without being insulted. I told them my odyssey while we drank coffee in the kitchen, but I was in constant fear that Joe might come in and find them there, and he hated them so much. I knew this wasn't a real possibility, but even so I was afraid. I was always afraid.

After he was in the hospital a while, they sent him home. He had to take two pills a day at a certain time, which I was in charge of giving him. I thought he'd have learned his lesson about drinking, but he kept right on. I think the drinks ruined the effect of the medicine. During one of the doctor's appointments I waited till Joe's attention was somewhere else and I told the doctor so. He was annoyed by this irresponsibility on the part of the patient, but Joe didn't care. Maybe he wanted to die.

He didn't work. He stayed in the house all day, cooked, and took care of my clothes and the boy's. He was always careful about details. One afternoon he came to one of my jobs to pick me up. I finished and got in the van. As soon as I sat down, he told me something so huge I couldn't believe it. The doctor had told him he had lung cancer. The cause was, Joe said, the number of X rays he'd had because of the tuberculosis. I cried, yelled, and insulted him because I knew this was the end.

"Why did you drink and smoke so much? Why didn't you listen to me?" He didn't say anything.

Sometimes I think it all happened because of his mother's death a little while after we got married. In the funeral parlor his sister told him it was his fault that their mother had died. I never understood what she meant because I never spoke to her or visited her again, and he didn't allow me to visit her, but after the funeral he drank and smoked more.

Realizing he was very sick, he decided to acquire my residency in this country. For years he'd accused me of having married him to get it, which is why he never filed the papers or let me file them. We'd been married twelve years. I chose a lawyer from the newspaper, the fastest one, and we went to what in those days I called the "Chinese Street," in lower Manhattan. The lawyer criticized him for having made me lose so much time. He said now it was as if I'd just arrived. "Why did you do that?" he asked. Joe answered that he thought since he was a citizen I'd get it automatically. The liar knew full well that it wasn't like that.

After he had an operation, his illness got worse. First they cut out one piece of his lung, then another, and then more operations after that. In the end I was the one who bathed him, changed his clothes, everything. I put down the toilet seat and sat him there to comb his hair just like I did with my son. Then he lay down in bed and I shaved him. I got to be an expert in that type of care. First I'd apply hot cloths, then shaving cream, then shave his beard. Things got worse and worse. The pain was so bad he couldn't sleep. I had to sleep in the living room with my son. Even the slightest movement in the bed bothered him. One morning he sent me to the hospital to exchange the sedatives he was using for some stronger ones. The nurse told me those were the strongest.

In spite of all that, they wouldn't hospitalize him. They said there was nothing more they could do. At night he called out for me all the time. Late one of those nights, when I was driven to desperation by his moans, I decided to talk with the doctor, go see him, break down crying in front of him, whatever I had to do, and beg that they take Joe back in the hospital again. One day I'd find him dead when I got home from work, I thought.

I succeeded in getting him admitted. I remember so clearly the moment he left for the hospital. He sat on the edge of the bed and took out his wallet. I looked at it, thinking how I'd never touched it. He gave me his Social Security card and union card and told me these were the places that would send me money when he was gone. He asked me to forgive him for never having filed for my residency and for the fact that I hadn't been able to go see my mother in the fourteen years since I came here. He said the problem was that he'd always tried to protect me, and really he'd overprotected me. The last thing he said was, "Forgive me for having done you so much harm." We walked into the kitchen because he wanted a little coffee before he left, and there he told me how much he loved me and that he knew this was the end. He was going to die, and he'd be waiting for me over there. He asked me to observe a mourning period of a year and then to get married, because it wasn't good for a woman to be alone the way his mother had been.

While he was telling me this, I thought to myself, "I'm not getting married again."

We took a taxi and brought the boy, as always, since I never had a sitter. They admitted Joe. The doctor said he didn't know how long he was going to live, you never could say. He was strong, and there would be improvements and relapses. Only God knew. I went to visit every day, what a struggle, from work to home to the hospital, with the boy in tow, and to top it off the rules said no minors were allowed. Since he was only eleven, they often didn't let him in. Then I had to find a way to leave him downstairs so that I could go up, or sneak him upstairs when I had a chance. Since the nurses knew I was good at taking care of sick people, they didn't bother with Joe's room when I was there. I fed him and washed him after he did his business. Whenever an I.V. bag ran out, I closed the little knob that let the liquid into his vein, detached the bag, took it to the nurses' station, brought back a new one, hung it on the stand, and opened the knob carefully so that the right amount would drip through. Sometimes I regulated the oxygen tank, opening or closing its valve so that more or less would come out when he felt uncomfortable. The nurses and even the doctors adored me. Sometimes I gave them a hand with other patients.

I only cried when I was alone with the boy and full of fear. I felt like the living dead; I was afraid to be in my house, I don't know why. One night Monica and I ate *ceviche* and *papas a la huancaina* that she brought over. When she saw what a mess I was, and the bags under my eyes from not sleeping, she gave me a steady look and said, "Elena, what are you crying over, what do you miss? The torture?" But I couldn't help feeling bad about his fate. Nobody is all bad. When he wasn't drinking, he was good. I'm not covering up for him or defending him; I'm just trying to tell the truth.

In one of his moments of relief I asked whether he had registered the land under my name. I asked that because I'd watched him, drunk, sending only his name to go on the deed. I didn't appear in it, even though we were married. Now he said that he had, and I shouldn't worry. In a little while Monica and Yokasta arrived to visit him. They came every so often, more to keep me company. Since it was a great effort for Joe to speak and he could barely move, most of the time he didn't know he had visitors. If he wasn't asleep, he'd see them come in and close his eyes, exhausted. I told them my concern about the deed to the house upstate. I was afraid, and not just about the cabin. Since my name didn't appear on any document, I thought they might take away the apartment where I lived if my husband wasn't living there anymore. Monica and Yokasta told me that wasn't possible. To put me at ease and to assure us all of the truth, a few days later they took me to see a lawyer. He told us that Joe had never put the house under my name. With only his name appearing on the deed, I'd have to divide it with the five children from his first marriage. That hurt me a lot, and I cried endlessly. Monica and Yokasta cursed and insulted him.

His ex-wife arranged to see me in the hospital lobby, where

she appeared with her twins. She wanted her part of the land. "Why are you doing this to me," I demanded, "when I'm the one who's suffered with him to the end?"

"You're young and can marry again," she answered. "Marry a rich man. We're not to blame for what you went through. We've been through a lot ourselves." They left and I never saw them again.

I went up to Joe's room, where he was having trouble breathing. I checked the valve on the oxygen tank to see whether there was a problem, but everything looked normal. While I was checking this, Monica and Yokasta arrived. I told them how bad Joe looked and we talked about my meeting with his ex-wife. We were standing there talking, and they said we ought to go sit and have coffee in the hospital restaurant instead. They had just gotten off work and were tired. Joe's breathing got more labored. I bent over the valve of the oxygen tank to open it a bit, but instead of turning it to the left, I turned it to the right, toward the closed position. I felt it reach the point where it wouldn't turn anymore. I tightened it a little bit, then more firmly, all without interrupting my conversation with Monica and Yokasta. Then I straightened up and we went to the restaurant.

I ordered macaroni with chicken and a salad, because I was hungry and wouldn't be getting home till late. The boy was with my sister-in-law, whom I was in touch with again. About forty-five minutes went by. The cafeteria was closing and they were telling visitors it was time to leave.

We went back upstairs to say good-bye to Joe. It was so silent there. I hadn't heard him sleep so peacefully in a long time. I went up to the oxygen tent he was lying under and saw that his eyelids were almost closed, with just a little sliver of eye showing. His head was to one side and a fine thread of saliva hung from his mouth and ran down onto the pillow. Monica and Yokasta came over. "He's in peace, don't bother him," they said. I was in a daze, digesting the macaroni after not eating for many hours, tired from my long day of work, my bad night, my bad life. I wasn't thinking, only acting. I slowly put on my coat and started walking toward the door. I'd completely forgotten having closed the oxygen. Everything was so strange. Yokasta, with her purse in her hand and ready to leave, asked me to wait a minute. She set down the purse on the only chair in the room, went to the tank, leaned over, and turned the valve toward the left. I could see the effort she made to open it, from the tightening of her nose and mouth. She put her purse over her shoulder and the three of us left the hospital.

It was almost ten at night, starting to cool off. We walked to the subway in silence, not speaking ill of Joe as we usually did. More than ten years have gone by since then. We see each other all the time and no one has ever mentioned that incident, and we are so talkative, such storytellers. In all honesty, I've come to seriously question whether it was real. I was so tired...

The hospital called me at work, early, to inform me that he had died the night before, without pain. I cried a lot over him. I was terribly indignant about the doctor putting such stress on the fact that he'd died without pain. Pain or no pain, he was dead. I went home and told my closest neighbors the news. I called the school to let them know what had happened. The principal said that if I wanted, he would send the boy right home. I said they should let him stay until school let out, and made coffee for Monica, Yokasta, and myself. We drank it in silence, in peace, without my worrying that somebody would come and interrupt us.

Now that you know the story, tell me, ma'am. Seeing how good I was to him and how much I loved him in spite of everything, do you believe I could have been capable of disconnecting the machine, and that my friends could have helped me? Don't you think the pain and suffering could have made me imagine that terrible event?

You're right, there's no way you could know.

Lunacy

I hope you don't mind my bringing this outline to guide me through my story. When I talk, I feel more secure if I have something in writing to hang on to. I had a hard time preparing it, because I don't remember much about my childhood, and I've spent days delving into remote corners of my memory. But I think I've managed to put down what I set out to get: accurate information and a succinct recounting of the important events in my development as a person. I'll be brief. As a good mathematician, I'm precise and don't like to digress.

Let me say that it's been more than twenty years since I've slept with a woman. It's always men, and black ones. Or at least men of color, by the standards of this country. Whites don't appeal to me sexually. I know where this comes from. What I don't know about is the other thing that I'll talk about later.

I'll start with my origins. I was born in a small town of Havana Province where they grow wonderful potatoes and citrus fruits, time moves slowly, and nothing happens. We were away from the coast, so there wasn't even boat traffic. Luckily, an irrigation channel connected to the Mayabeque River ran right through the yard of my house, which provided my childhood with some relief, and besides, in its clear waters I learned to swim. My father was the town doctor, my mother the pharmacist, and together they owned and ran the only decent drugstore in the area.

The great annual event was the arrival, each July, of a circus with its tattered tent. The main attractions were a toothless lion and the Platinum Woman, always newly returned from a European *tournée*, according to the ringmaster, who also served as orchestra and ticket seller. He was an old, skinny man, who played the congas when his wife came on stage to dance the rumba. He also played the violin for his daughter's trapeze act and did the drum roll to announce the entrance of the Platinum Woman, most likely his lover. She would stride quickly to the center of the ring wearing a flowered bikini and swiveling her hips in time to the music, which made her conspicuous belly bounce along. Her belly was covered with stretch marks around a protruding navel, suggesting many pregnancies. She owed her stage name to her hair, dyed platinum blond. Her act consisted of singing boleros—horribly—in imitation of Olga Guillot and María Luisa Landín. The whole spectacle seems pathetic when I recall it now, but at the time these performances got me so worked up I couldn't even swallow a mouthful of the meal before the circus.

Second, I'll tell you about my upbringing. I am an only child and have been asthmatic from birth, so I grew up pampered and spoiled. I even had a nursemaid almost into my adolescence. When I was eight, Teresita was still giving me baths. She was a big girl who took care of me from soon after I was born. The truth is, I had nothing against that. I can still recall my feeling of pleasure after the bath, heading toward the bed in her arms, wrapped in a huge towel. Neither the towel nor the girl may have been as immense as I remember, but that's how they lodged in my imagination. She would put me to bed and there I'd stay for a while, naked, wrapped in the softness of terry cloth until I was "normalized," a mysterious expression used by my grandmother on my mother's side. Teresita accompanied me under the towel in this process, her body warm and broad and me like a little lizard folded into her breast and thighs. We'd sleep that way for fifteen or twenty minutes. My mother or one of my grandmothers—both lived in the house—would make the rounds frequently to be sure their orders were being carried out. I would peek out through my eyelashes enough to glimpse their shadowy beatific faces smiling at this placid scene. The family adored this maid, principally on account of her skill in managing my nap, until one day it dawned on them that her belly was more swollen than her good appetite could account for, and they fired her.

I cried a lot when she left. A lot. I tried to prevent it, but my begging was of no use. They thought I was too innocent to know why she was being fired, but I knew better, because Teresita had often spoken to me about her boyfriend, and I was precocious enough to guess what she didn't say. From the time they fired her, I refused to "normalize," which made all of them cry. I didn't care. Without Teresita's warmth it wasn't any fun.

While she was still there, at the end of the nap she would sit on the edge of the bed, place my feet on her skirt, and one by one she would powder the spaces between my toes with Mennen talc. Then, very calmly, she'd get me into my socks and shoes. That's how it was every morning before lunch, from as far back as I can remember. All that time everyone marveled over my docility about the bath. In fact that was the nicest time of all my interminable days as a pampered child brought up in the days before Nintendo games. Years later I realized that Teresita's dedication was due in part to the fact that drawing out our morning ritual exempted her for a while from heavier domestic tasks.

They watched me so carefully and took me for such a fragile child that I couldn't go around barefoot even at noon on suffocating summer days. I pleaded to be allowed to, while I angrily watched Teresita's wide naked feet sliding with delight over the cool black and white tiles of our big living room, which would be shining from their recent cleaning by Otilia, a solitary woman with long gray braids who had grown old as the servant of our family.

When it rained, unlike other children, I could never cool off my head under the deafening stream of clear water pouring down from the zinc gutter lining the tiled porch roof, where the summer downpours collected and ran into the yard. Furious, shut up in my room with the curtains closed, I tried to ignore the fun the others were having. But I could hear them running and laughing, and it hurt.

To my mother, even an innocent daytime drizzle was capable of unleashing the whistling in my chest by the time night fell. "The whistling in your chest" was another mystery in the family lexicon that my grandmothers repeated by my sickbed while I meditated on the phrase and struggled to breathe through congested and sleepless nights.

I lived surrounded by prohibitions. The ones about food were the worst. I loved green mangos, but God protect me from eating them. In ascending and inevitable order would come indigestion, diarrhea, high fever, and typhus.

But the worst taboo was fish. Before serving me fish, they ground it up to get rid of any bones. Once this process was finished, when all trace of its original preparation was gone, the fish would be brought to me turned into an aseptic, discolored mess, saturated with phosphorus, they said, and good for my brain. The adults ate fried fish, fish in tomato sauce, fish in green sauce, breaded fish, or leftover fish refried. But mine always came beaten to death. Its nauseating appearance kept me from even trying it.

How could I find it anything but disgusting, since I knew the tasteless mush they put in front of me had been worked over by at least twenty fingers? First the cook, author of a meticulous search, plunging her ten fingers into the fish's flesh more out of fear of my mother's wrath than of my choking, and then my mother, dismembering it centimeter by centimeter to assure herself that no vestige of a bone remained. Sometimes there was a third and even a fourth inspection by my grandmothers. It was truly disgusting.

I don't want you to misinterpret my relationship with my mother, whom I loved very much and admired as well. She was probably the only woman in the whole town with a college degree. Besides, she was generous and giving. Sensitive to the pain of others. The servants loved her. She was especially close to the cook, a single mother with a son just two years older than me, though it seemed more like five or six. His name was Genaro and he practically lived in my house. Between his strength and his mischief he came to be nicknamed Sandokan, after the character on the radio serial based on the Emilio Salgari book. A live wire, my mother called Genaro. From the first time I heard that phrase—live wire—I would repeat it to myself during the downpours as I sat on my bed listening to him running wild under the rain, brandishing a wooden sword that the Magi had left for him at my house, while I received educational toys.

But what left an indelible mark on me were the nights I'd leave the dining room crying after being scolded for not having eaten and I'd see Sandokan seated at the kitchen table, where he and his mother ate, enjoying a whole fish, head and all. I would lean against the doorframe, simply amazed to watch how he ate everything on his plate including the eyes and brains, which he sucked happily, extracting them from the tiny bones of the skull. Sometimes he would begin to eat off of a plate one of the adults had left, picking at bits of flesh among the bones that had been left untouched. He swallowed these with pleasure, without the slightest worry that a bone might get stuck on a tonsil and he'd have to be rushed to the hospital to have it removed, just like my mother and grandmothers said could happen to me. Enraptured, I watched him chew. Once in while he would pull a large fishbone from his mouth and set it on the edge of the plate, or else two or three small bones would emerge all at once from between his lips. The first time I saw this scene, I was about nine, because it was soon after they fired Teresita. I asked my mother why they served fish with bones to him but not to me. "Because he can eat them," she answered in a tone full of mystery and fascination to my ears. Her comment confirmed several of my old suspicions. The cook's son was a superboy while I was a runt, as my schoolmates would yell on the few occasions I tried to fight with anyone. Poor me. I spent my childhood under a cloud, missing Teresita and envying Sandokan.

Third, I'll talk about my move to Havana and my first homosexual experience.

When I finished elementary school, my parents were worried that there wasn't a good high school in the town, so they sent me to an aunt's house on Calle Monserrate, in Old Havana, where I could pursue my studies at the Havana Institute. It was their idea—I even resisted at first—but they had suddenly decided that my education was paramount. They almost forced me to go. I passed from an overprotected childhood to an almost completely independent adolescence, far from my mother's tutelage. At first it was hard. I was shy and had trouble making friends. Nonetheless, in spite of the city's soot and of sleeping in a poorly ventilated room, my asthma and food allergies disappeared. I had two girlfriends during that time, though I was never very enthusiastic about them. At their initiative I had a few sexual encounters that were both reluctant and incomplete. I did it more to stay in good standing with my friends than for my own pleasure.

I didn't fall in love until I entered college and met Armando. We shared a room in a rooming house in Vedado. He was the son of a dentist and an elementary school teacher, and from the provinces like me. We started the same year, he in architecture and I in math.

He was quiet and studious, an introverted person with long lashes and big eyes. Right from the beginning I found his company enormously attractive, and soon I realized that he reminded me of Sandokan. I spent a few days mulling over this association. There was no physical resemblance, nor did their personalities match. Besides, their upbringings were quite the opposite. One night as we drank our coffee after dinner, we began to flirt in a subtle way, and that's when I realized that it was the brown tone of his skin that made me associate him with Sandokan. Since that time that's been the color of love for me. We became lovers. It wasn't a problem for me to discover I was attracted by my own sex. Maybe I subconsciously suspected it, I don't know. I think my marginalization as a child prepared me to accept my sexuality. Of course, I'm making a short summary out of a long thought process. For example, coming from such a restricted childhood, there's no way I could be speaking with you so openly if I hadn't been in therapy since I got to this country. Conclusively accepting that I'm a homosexual and coming out of the closet the way I've done has not been so easy. And now I'm confused all over again, when I thought I was so sure of who I was.

To complete my story, I'll tell you about Matthew and what I think of as the dark side of my eroticism. I've lived with him for six years. I met him through an ad I put in the personals section of the paper where Rodolfo, a friend of mine, has worked for many years. Whenever I have to advertise anything, I do it there. It was Rodolfo who told me about you, one Friday afternoon over some beers. While we were drinking he told me about his strange attraction to a neighbor with an unbearable smell. That's how I got the idea of coming to you.

Many people find it strange that someone with my social position and seriousness would resort to that means of finding a partner, but the explanation is simple. I got tired of the accidental way you meet someone at a party, at work or through common friends. You meet like that, and little by little you discover your differences in tastes, interests, and even values. Several times I've begun a romance with a friend, and then when he ran into trouble I found myself without a lover or a friend. Enough of that, I said. I hadn't been lucky with recent partners and I was running out of friends. I decided to go after unknown people, to interview candidates, to give them a question-naire to fill out and see whether we had real affinities or not. I did it, and it worked. With fifty-four responses in a single week, I was bound to find what I was looking for. That's why I believe in planning.

But there's something else beyond my understanding, and I hate it when I don't understand. For you to grasp the rest, I have to tell you that I've never had an excessive sexual appetite. I'm tranquil by nature, or so I thought until now. Matthew, on the other hand, has a fiery temperament. It's the only way we're dissimilar, which I knew from his question-naire, but of all fifty-four people I interviewed he was the most compatible with my personality. From the beginning of our relationship he tried various methods to increase my desire, without much result. After we'd been together for two years—that was three years ago—his frustration grew to the point where it threatened our relationship, solid as it was in every other way. The situation gave me many sleepless nights.

One afternoon Matthew came home from work with a bag full of pornographic films of all different subjects and styles for me to choose the ones that excited me. I was moved by his zeal to resolve our problem, so I accepted the suggestion, although without much hope. Even so, I devoted long hours over the next few days to my selection. It was a desperate measure after a series of situations too humiliating and intimate for me to describe. I'd never been enthusiastic about gay erotic films, but to my astonishment and Matthew's satisfaction, I've suddenly become an excellent lover. Using a film as the starting point for making love has become a ritual with us, and now I take to the task with a fiery heat. The change is incredible. So incredible that I keep watching Matthew's movies that so he won't dis-cover the truth, which is that those aren't the ones that do it for me. It's the others, which I buy in secret and watch alone before he comes home. The scenes from these films throb in my memory while we're in bed and give me strength. I hide them in the basement among some old science books. They're all heterosexual—that's my secret. I have an enormous collection, and always, invariably, over the past three years, I've arrived at the climactic moment of lovemaking with my partner by imagining myself penetrating one of those women. The hunger with which I possess them in my mind translates into action in bed, action Matthew interprets as passion for him. Speaking with complete honesty, I could be with any man, even a stranger, and I'd act with the same passion. The erotic object is a vagina that lives in my head.

At first these fantasies amused me, but by now they've gotten too strong not to take them seriously. They worry me. It's exhausting not to have an orgasm, not a single one, without being immersed in a scene that in reality is unknown to me. Lately the fantasies have begun to spring up anytime and anywhere, sometimes in the middle of solving a problem in math. For the past few days I've been playing with the idea of putting an ad in the personals, in the same paper where I put the one that brought Matthew to me. If I were more daring, less shy, I'd do it, but I don't think I'll take the risk. I've been gay all my life and wouldn't even know what to do if I found myself in a real situation like that. It's lunacy, I know, but I desire these women like I've never desired anyone in my life. Doesn't that sound strange to you?

Catching On

"Cowardly love goes nowhere,
comes to nothing."
—*Silvio Rodríguez*

One night, when I was seventeen, I dreamed I was making love with a woman. She was naked and her body was quite beautiful. Even today I remember her firm, full breasts and her skin that shined with a color like that of tobacco.

I found the dream very disturbing. In those days, the mid 1950s, I was seeing a psychologist because I was getting depressed often without knowing why. He was a single man around fifty years old who praised me frequently during my visits to his office. I told him my dream. He asked me if I had ever thought about "that." I imagined that "that" meant homosexual ideas and I answered in the negative. The way he posed the question, avoiding having to speak directly, did not encourage deeper exploration of this topic. He told me not to worry; the dream symbolized something else. His professional opinion calmed me and I tried to forget the whole matter. Nevertheless, in the days that followed, every time I hugged my boyfriend I wondered despite myself what the smooth, taut skin of the woman in my dream would really feel like.

In the summer of 1969 I came to live in New York with my
husband and our daughters. It had been a long time since I'd
had that disturbing dream and I'd put it out of my mind. Or so
I thought. The girls were now old enough to go to school, the
house was suffocating me, and we needed more money than
what my husband was earning. His poor English prevented
him, at the time, from practicing his profession. Recommended
by some friends, I got work in a small office on Irving Place,
near Union Square. They didn't pay well, but I hardly had to
speak any English and for me that was an absolute require-
ment. I took the job as something temporary. I detested office
work, but didn't know what else to do. All I was sure of was
that I loved my daughters a lot and that I couldn't stand
spending my life doing domestic chores.

I started work on a Monday at the beginning of autumn. On
my way to the office that rainy morning I imagined I would be
exhausted by the end of the afternoon. I had gotten up at five
to make breakfast, leave the house tidy, and take the girls to
school. A woman from the neighborhood would pick them up
and take care of them until I got back.

I rode the elevator in the building where my job was, thinking that I should have made myself up better for my first day
of work, but I hadn't felt like it. My boss, a short, fat man of
Irish descent, greeted me and escorted me to the room where
I'd be working. I knew that there weren't many employees in
the office, but I never imagined that there would only be three
of us. The first I saw was a tall, olive-skinned woman who was
standing next to a large window, looking out onto the park that
faced the building, drinking her tea distractedly. She wore a
blouse with long sleeves and a pleated skirt that had been
ironed with great care. She had black, shoulder-length hair,
which she parted on the right. The boss called her over to introduce her to me.

When she turned to us, I noticed her broad cheeks, her
slightly large mouth, and her narrow lips, but above all, her
eyes. They were very dark, fairly small, almond-shaped, and

they seemed to remain serious even when she smiled, as she was doing now, walking over with a cup in her hand. Months later, when I was no longer in touch with her, that image from our first meeting kept coming to my mind. She told me her name was Zobeida. I told her mine, and we complimented each other on our names.

There were still a few minutes before we were supposed to begin work. Zobeida asked if I wanted tea or coffee. As there were only the three of us working there, the company offered it to us for free. She liked tea with milk. I never drank tea but told her I'd have the same. She poured two cups and we sat side by side in the seats where we would work for the next eight hours. The tea with milk became a sort of ritual we would practice all day long. She would prepare it for me or I would prepare it for her.

We were doing the most boring work in the world. The good thing was that the boss never interrupted our conversations as long as we didn't slack on the work. The other employee sat facing us: a Romanian woman about forty years old, tall and blond, also recently arrived in the States. A talker, she told us how in Romania she had lived on the main street of Bucharest in a spacious apartment with a large balcony overlooking the street. In New York she lived in a room with a single window looking onto the building's central airshaft. Every day she would complain about having come here. She considered herself a beauty and had expected that a millionaire would be waiting for her at the airport with a marriage proposal. But he still hadn't shown up and she was starting to lose her patience. Zobeida and I were also becoming impatient with her interminable story. We opted to appear so involved in our work that finally she closed her mouth. Zobeida and I began speaking in Spanish. We hit it off right away. By the afternoon of that first work day we knew we had a lot in common. We were both Cuban, so the first thing we talked about was the island. Then, too, Zobeida was almost my age, married as well and with two boys about the same age as my girls. We both liked books, music, movies. When I got home that afternoon, I thought to myself that it had been friendship at first sight. I told my husband how nice she was and went to bed excited at the prospect of resuming our conversation the next day.

From the very beginning Zobeida inspired in me a feeling that was strange yet familiar, so I didn't think about it much. Familiar because in order to feel happy, I had always needed the intimate friendship of a woman. To a certain extent this was normal in my culture, but in my case the need was very strong. I knew women for whom their husbands were their whole world and their girlfriends only supplements, replaceable, pleasant relationships but something they could do without. It's never been like that for me. Since I was little, I've needed to share what I've been thinking and feeling and some of what I'm doing with another woman. One of my great pleasures was to sit and drink coffee and talk easily and intimately with a woman friend. Nevertheless Zobeida, for some reason I couldn't put my finger on, left me uneasy. She made me like and trust her as other women had in the past, but the feeling was more intense. This intensity was what made me uneasy.

Zobeida also felt it was very important to have women friends. So much so that it was the cause of one of the greatest problems she'd had with her mother when she was eighteen and engaged to a boy. She had a girlfriend to whom she was very attached and whom she'd known since before meeting her boyfriend. Once, Zobeida got sick and was in bed for several days and the only person she wanted to see was her girlfriend. Her mother was so worried about her preference that she asked her daughter if they were anything more than friends. As far as Zobeida was concerned, her mother was nuts, but the woman insisted on knowing the truth. She made her daughter kneel down before her and swear she wasn't lying. Zobeida remembered that story as the most humiliating moment in her life. I asked her why she preferred to be with her girlfriend than with her fiancé. She said that she felt less alone with her.

In a few short days we had told each other our lives: where

our parents and grandparents were born, our experiences giving birth, the sicknesses our children had had. We both considered our stay in New York to be only temporary. We didn't think the city was a good place to raise children. We wanted somewhere more peaceful, houses with more space. Her husband and mine were both looking for work in other states and in Latin America.

As the days passed, after we had told what we had lived through, we went on to analyze why things had happened as they did. We began to talk about our feelings and from that point on we hardly switched topics. We weren't happy. Both of us were having marital problems. Nevertheless, according to the standards of our culture, both her husband and mine were beyond reproach. They kept no lovers, didn't drink, didn't hit us, and were good providers. Zobeida's problem, she thought, was that she felt a large void stemming from her husband's indifference to sex in general, not just in their relationship. His sexual life was practically nonexistent. Nevertheless, she considered him to be intelligent and sensible, and they were good friends. Since getting married, she had had a lover, but that didn't work out either. She wished to share her life with a man with whom she was in love. My problem was different. My husband and I didn't live in different worlds, we lived in different galaxies. We were having sexual difficulties at that time. Not because of sex in and of itself but because of a lack of mutual understanding.

We told each other of our past loves. My favorite boyfriend had been my first, when I was fourteen years old. Zobeida's best relationship was with her fiancé from when she was eighteen, even though she didn't want to see him when she got sick. She said that he was a sensitive boy and a good guitarist. At this point in the story, we commented on how incredible it was that both of us were nearly thirty and still hadn't found a man who made us happy. "A woman as good-looking as you," I said. "As you," Zobeida said. And so we praised each other as we complained. When we were done with men past and present, we turned to men of the future. We both thought that at some point we would get divorced and find the man who would make us happy. Then we sang each other's praises again. Two women as attractive as we were deserved to lead happy lives.

From the second day on, we chose not to go out to eat. We would bring something from home and eat in the office. We didn't have much money, and furthermore the lunch hour was the best time to talk. Our boss and the other employee would leave. They'd say they needed a little air after four hours of being cooped up in here, but for us it was more important to have time alone. It was during our lunch hour that we could pay full attention to each other's stories. After a few days we were almost completely isolated from Charlotte, who always sat across the table from us. To such a degree that she began to feel jealous because there was no one to listen to her stories. With the passage of every day, without realizing it, we spoke to each other in ever-lower voices and sat closer and closer together. While we worked, without looking at each other, we would talk for long periods of time about books, movies, and a hundred other things. But sometimes, when the topic was ourselves and we came to a particularly happy or sad point in the story, we would put down the lists we were checking over and look each other straight in the eye. That's when my heart would beat faster and stronger. Our conversation was getting me overwrought, I'd think. What could I do, since I couldn't speak of my feelings and sorrows with anyone else? It was logical that I'd get excited.

Four or five weeks after we had started working, now in October, I was standing one morning in front of the bathroom mirror about to apply my makeup. My resistance to getting dressed up and putting on my face had vanished. I was waking up full of enthusiasm, thinking about what I'd wear and what color lipstick would go best with my clothes. I finished doing my lipstick and examined myself in the mirror to see how I looked. I was content, eager to leave. Suddenly, as I looked myself in the eyes, I heard a question that came unexpectedly and sounded as if someone else were asking it, as if the woman inside the mirror were asking the one outside: "Why are you taking such care in dressing and making yourself up?" A second question followed immediately: "Who are you dressing and making yourself up for?" I heard the answer in a voice that wasn't mine although it came from me: "For Zobeida." I was paralyzed. No, I couldn't be making myself up for another woman. And yet it was true. Suddenly I remembered the dream I'd had when I was seventeen. Could the psychologist have got it wrong and the dream did indeed have to do with sexual desire? Might I be a homosexual? The thought tormented me like you wouldn't believe. I felt something come loose inside my head and begin to spin crazily around. I couldn't think straight. My knowledge of sexual relations between women was limited to the story in a pornographic paperback that had fallen into my hands when I was a teenager and the rumors I'd heard about how, in some of the clubs in Havana, American tourists paid famous mambo dancers to go to bed together while they watched. I had never heard or read about love between women. The "female inverts" that came up now and then in family conversation seemed as foreign to me as Martian women.

In any case, I went to work that morning. I calmed down after a while and on the train ride decided it wasn't such a big deal. Even in the worst of cases, no one knew what I was thinking or feeling. I've always striven to be honest with myself, so I decided to face my feelings. The first thing was to try to define what it was I felt for Zobeida. That we hit it off excellently, that we got along well, and that I felt real companionship with her, of those things I had no doubt. But all of that was fine. For me the line dividing friendship and love was whether I wanted to sleep with her. That, which I'd never considered before, was what I had to find out. I probably did want her unconsciously, I thought to myself.

I got to the office and said hello to Zobeida, as I did every day. A short while later she asked what was wrong. Nothing, I was fine, I answered. I spent that day and the following ones watching her and asking myself whether I wanted to make love with her. I looked at her mouth when she spoke or laughed and wondered what it would feel like if I kissed her or if she kissed me. I could not imagine myself kissing her. After interrogating myself obsessively, always coming up with the same answer, I convinced myself that that wasn't what I wanted. After endless meditations, Romain Rolland, the French author, came to my rescue. I remembered his phrase that friendship is a romance between souls. That's what this was, and I had nothing to feel guilty about. From then on, we got closer every day.

In the afternoon we would always walk to the train together and then go our separate ways at the station. But one day it occurred to us to go shopping for fifteen or twenty minutes, no longer, since we were always in a hurry to get home. I told the neighbor who took care of the girls that the trains were a mess, that I would pay her overtime when I was late. I told my husband, who always got home after I did, the same story. Zobeida spoke with her mother, who looked after her kids, and told her something similar. We hardly ever bought anything. We'd go from store to store, consulting one another on matters of taste and price, and talking. It gradually became more and more difficult for us to part. We stretched the twenty minutes to half an hour.

I arrived one morning to find Zobeida, who generally got there before me, sipping tea by the large window as she had been on the first day. It was Friday and we wouldn't see each other over the weekend. I walked over to her and told her that something had occurred to me on the way to work. Without hesitating, she responded, "That when we leave this afternoon, we go sit for a while in the park." I stared at her, flabbergasted. We had never sat in the park. I couldn't believe that she'd said exactly what I was thinking, before I'd even said a word. I answered, "How did you know?" Looking me in the eyes, she said, "Do you know you're frightening me?"

From that day on, we went to the park instead of the stores. We never bought anything anyway, and in the park we could talk more comfortably. We spoke about the same topics as always and of our small achievements in our daily lives, but our conversations were becoming more difficult, with frequent silences during which we would look into each other's eyes for a few seconds and then shift our gaze to the trees that were losing their leaves, or we would make some comment about the beautiful autumn color that was covering the grass and sidewalks. Little by little we left off talking about our husbands, about men in general, about books, movies, about our homes and even our children. At times we would sit there next to each other without saying a word for several minutes. I wanted to be with her, be with her, be with her. Nothing else mattered to me but being with her. Why? I couldn't come up with an answer. I often felt an urge to cry. The same thing was happening to her. So we thought it was the state of our marriages, heading from bad to worse. We had to find a solution, find a man to fall in love with, we concluded.

Instead of looking for men, we began to visit each other on Sundays. Sometimes I would go to her house with my daughters and husband and sometimes she would come to mine with her family entourage. It was now November. Even though it was starting to get too cold to sit in the park, and no one was out there, the two of us kept on. Even the bums and drug addicts grew scarce, but we showed up every afternoon and always lingered a few more minutes before parting. I started to think that I didn't even love my daughters because it was on their account that I had to go home early. Still, I kept working, doing the household chores and giving my husband a peck on the cheek when he got home.

Around the end of that month Zobeida's husband was notified that he had been accepted for a job in northern Florida. It would start at the beginning of December. They would be leaving after Thanksgiving. Since we had no idea where we would end up in the future, she said, with destinies as uncertain as ours were, we should think of a way to guarantee that if we lost contact, we could find each other again. I would call an aunt of hers who'd been living in New York for many years. This woman would tell me where to find Zobeida.

On her last Friday at work, at the end of the day, I rode the train with her to her station. Standing there, facing one another in silence as she was about to get off, and without having spoken until then, she said, "I've been thinking about this a lot, and I believe that it's better that I go, because if I don't, this is going to get more complicated." We didn't even kiss the way Cuban women friends kiss, rubbing cheeks without our mouths intervening. She squeezed my shoulder with her hand by way of farewell and we stared at each other until the train doors opened. At that moment I felt, yes, I clearly felt that I didn't want her to leave like that, without us embracing, without our hands being able to touch the skin of the other at least once. I felt my heart beating in my throat, that I was about to start sobbing deeply, but I didn't. I stayed on the train, heading for my house, repeating silently to myself those last words and feeling that farewell squeeze in my shoulder.

I haven't seen Zobeida since. I hear that she got divorced, remarried, and then went back to her first husband. I don't know what she's thinking nowadays or whether she remembers our afternoons in the park. I'd like to ask her.

Adela's Lovely Eyes

I came to New York in 1966, when the Vietnam War was on. In those days you showed up at a factory, said "I want a job," and right away they sat you down or stood you up in front of a machine you'd never seen before and had no idea how to work. And you started packaging screwdrivers or sausages.

Within a few months of arriving in the United States, I'd had jobs in two factories, one where they sewed clothes and the other where they packaged labels with first names printed on them: Mary, Betty, Carolyn, a ton of names in English. People put the labels inside the collars of their blouses. When the official at Immigration got me the first job, she warned the company manager that I'd never used a commercial sewing machine before. "That doesn't matter," the man said. "We'll teach her, she'll learn."

Confident and happy, I started on a Monday, sure that very soon I'd learn to operate the machinery. It was a men's clothing factory. Almost before I got my coat off, a tall man with his gray hair combed like in Hollywood movies from the forties handed me several hundred pairs of long, narrow, slightly curved strips of cloth. My work would be to join each pair to make the collar of an overcoat. He showed me where to sit and which buttons started and stopped the machine. He mumbled something in English and left. I didn't understand but thought maybe he'd said, "Have a nice day."

I started working on the strips of cloth and sewed them together, but they didn't look anything like the collar of an overcoat. It was harder than I'd figured. Very upset, I looked around every so often in search of help. But my lack of English made it hard for me to communicate with the other women, and they were too busy to notice the suffering on my face. I kept on trying to stitch the pieces together. Once in a while I stopped working and watched the skilled woman alongside me piling up ten or twelve well-made collars in the time it took me to finish a single disastrous one.

In spite of the time pressure, at lunchtime two or three women came over to offer me some encouragement, to tell me that the first week was the worst, that I'd feel much better after that. When I went back to work, the collars started to improve. By the end of the day I counted more than a hundred pieces that, if they weren't perfect, weren't so bad considering it was the first time in my life I ever did that kind of job.

The second day, I arrived even more pleased with myself, proud of the control I'd acquired over the machines the first day. When the foreman saw me, without saying hello or waiting for me to sit down, he asked me to come with him. He went to a table and came back holding a little bunch of collars in the palm of his hand. He showed them to me one by one, taking his time, and said, "Out of the hundred-some you made yesterday, those twenty-five are the only ones we can use. We had to throw out the rest." He handed me an envelope with ten dollars for the one day's work and left without giving me a chance to ask what happened to the training they'd promised. I wanted to say good-bye to the women who had tried to help me the day before, but I couldn't hold back my tears. I would have been ashamed for them to see me cry.

On the way to the door I heard one of them arguing with the foreman. "They didn't give her time to learn," she was telling the man. I don't know what he said back to her, because she was still talking when I left. Down in the street I kept on crying all the way to the subway. I felt humiliated, frustrated, and above all I felt powerless. The worst was the crying, which made me feel ridiculous. There were tons of jobs around, so it was no big deal. I got home, drank some coffee, and little by little stopped crying before the kids came home from school.

In the second factory everything went fine. There were only a few of us, the work was easy, and I even made a friend there, Zobeida. I got really fond of her, but the plant only operated during the summer and my friend moved to Washington, D.C., where her husband had been offered a good job.

Now it was September. I'd been out of work more than three weeks, and even though my husband had a relatively good job for someone who hadn't been here long, we needed my wages too. Searching for work wasn't exactly fun. Sometime they gave me dirty looks and I didn't know what they were saying to me. Every night I felt worse about getting up the next day to go about the same unpleasant task. Ever since I've been a girl, I've tried to take care of things myself as best I can, but this time I needed someone else.

One sleepless night I got up to get a drink of water. On my way to the refrigerator, about four in the morning, I thought of asking Adela to go with me. Why hadn't I thought of this before? She was my friend from childhood. She'd lived in New York for five years and never worked outside her house. I told her it would be good for her to go out, it would be a fantastic chance to practice her English too. That felt like a lie, since she still could barely speak it, which was why she stayed shut up in her house. But the factories of New York were full of Latinos, and it would be a relief for her to be able to speak Spanish with adults. She wouldn't have to spend her day correcting them the way she did with her six-year-old, who got his words mixed up all the time. She had nothing to lose by trying, and a lot to gain.

Adela wasn't happy about the idea. She didn't like working
in factories. Her mother-in-law and sister-in-law both worked
in a foundry, where it was hot as hell and they'd gone half deaf
from the sound of the machines. But she didn't know enough
English to get any other kind of job. I told her that it was just
temporary, that later we'd find something better for ourselves.
My closing argument, the most important point, was that her
marriage was falling apart. Although she was trying to save it,
there really wasn't much hope, and the best thing for her would
be to have some economic independence so that she could feel
more sure of herself. I convinced her to come with me.

One Friday morning we dropped our kids off at school and
went out in a torrential rain. Before we entered the first building, Adela told me we had to speak more properly. "'I want a
job' isn't very polite. From now on, we'll say 'I am looking for
a job.'" That's what we did.

Back in my apartment that afternoon, over coffee, we dis-
cussed the five offers we'd received. We considered a toy factory where they gave the workers a discount. Christmas was
coming, and they had good-quality musical instruments, especially trumpets and drums. The drawback was the location.
The subway ride would be more than an hour and then a
twenty-minute walk along beat-up streets with no sidewalks.
We'd made the walk that day at noon, after the rain had let up,
but it was still flooded most of the way. It wasn't easy. We
imagined what it would be like in the winter, coming and
going in the darkness of those short days. Finally we chose the
place closest to the building where we both lived. They only
paid $1.25 an hour, but for the two of us, both bringing up kids,
distance and transportation decided it.

Monday morning we showed up early, before the seven-
thirty starting time, at the cosmetics factory in an old building
in Astoria. They made a brand of lipstick, eye shadow, and nail
polish that was very popular, not just in the United States but
in Latin America too. We went in. As soon as the machinery got
going, the ear-splitting noise and chemical smells were unbear-

able. Adela looked at me with her lovely eyes, even bigger than usual. I knew. I thought about the deafness of her mother- and sister-in-law. Before she could open her mouth, I tried to cheer her up with something that really didn't even convince me. "Look at all these women working here. If they can stand it, we can too." I didn't want to be left by myself in that horrible place.

We each got a blue uniform, both the same size. Two of me would have fit into mine. They were supposed to have short sleeves, I guessed, but on me the sleeves hung below my elbows. The skirt reached to my ankles. It was depressing. I tried to console myself by thinking that it might look like a long dress with three-quarter sleeves. In fact I've always liked vintage clothes and costumes.

Each department had a forelady with a blue uniform just like ours, but the top supervisor had a white uniform that fit. She was big with short, almost white hair. Besides the hair and uniform she had white shoes and socks. We Latinas called her *la paloma*, the dove. She took a liking to me from day one. She smiled when we passed each other, and I responded very politely. My mother always said that a beautiful smile will open any door for a woman, and mine had brought me compliments ever since I was a child. Everybody said *la paloma* was a stubborn tyrant, but she was always nice to me until I gave notice. Then she got nasty.

Adela had to work next to a huge tank of acetone, while I packaged bottles of nail polish. I'd never done that work before. They showed me how. You had to put a dozen little bottles into a small box, close it, and when you had a bunch of full boxes, you put them in bigger boxes, made of cardboard, kept for this purpose in one corner of the room. Every worker had a notebook to write down how many she'd done. The forelady warned me that you had to finish a certain number every day to keep your job, though I didn't have to worry much the first day because they understood it was my training period. She also told me that she came by regularly to check the notebooks. She gave me a Number 2 pencil and my book.

The bell rang and we started in. In the time it took me to fill two of the little boxes, the other women finished three. An hour went by. My speed didn't increase even though I tried. I thought of the garment factory and what happened after my first day there. I needed this job. For a while, keeping on at the same speed, all I thought about was how to solve the problem. I didn't notice the sound of the machines, even though it was almost impossible to ignore. Then I realized that as soon as the little boxes were put inside the big ones, there was no way to know who had done what because they were all mixed together without any identification.

Right away I came up with a system that made me fast. When I'd filled three little boxes, I ran to the corner with them, put them in one of the big boxes, and back at my seat I noted four more in my book. This way it'll be hard to know how many I do, since I'll never build up a pile of full boxes at my side, I thought. Before the forelady could ask me why I was getting up so often, I told her that this was my system, this was the way it was done in my country. Since my rushing around gave an impression of speed, she accepted that explanation without any questions.

At nine thirty in the morning the bell sounded for break. Most of the women pulled bottles of juice out of their purses and drank at the benches where they sat all day. Neither Adela nor I had brought a snack. We rushed to get out of our uniforms and over to a coffee shop across the street. When we got back, we heard the bell ring again. The ten-minute break was over. The women settled back into their seats, returning from the only chance all morning to go to the bathroom. I sat down, put my coffee to one side, still untouched, and started working again.

When the forelady came by to check my book, she was surprised at my efficiency. I felt more secure, encouraged by her praise, and my speed increased. For every two little boxes I finished I wrote down four. I heard her tell *la paloma* in English, "She is really fast."

Lunchtime came, and I watched a big group of workers head

for the bathroom, carrying their bag lunches along. Since we didn't see anyplace to sit, Adela and I followed them. We came to a dilapidated bathroom with old, flaking wooden benches set up in front of the toilets. A swarm of women filled the seats right away, except that nobody took the empty space at the end of one bench, even though some were eating standing up. I sat there and started to take out my lunch. Before I could finish doing that, a woman of about fifty came over and said, "*Mira, mi hija*, I've been working in this factory for five years. Luckily I've never been laid off. I've always sat to eat where you're sitting now. That's my regular spot." I got up, thinking how awful it would be to spend five years eating lunch with the toilet doors opening and closing right in your face.

Adela and I sat on the floor in a corner. She started to protest about the acetone smell, how much it bothered her. Since she was a born complainer, I didn't pay much attention. While we were eating, a Latino girl with a bathing cap on her head, and so covered with powder you couldn't tell what color her eyelashes or eyebrows were, sat down beside us and started to talk. She worked in the room where they bottled talc. "You get ten cents more an hour and they give you this cap to keep your hair clean," she said, pointing her index finger at her head. Someone had warned her, she said, that she shouldn't work there for more than four months, because breathing talcum powder eight hours a day was bad for your lungs. But she'd been there two years. As she was leaving us, she told us her name: Ramona. I said I wouldn't forget, because I liked that name a lot.

When we got off work that afternoon, Adela's throat was so sore she couldn't swallow or speak. We went to the hospital, where the doctor told her she couldn't work for at least a week. The glands in her neck were inflamed because of the acetone fumes. All the way home she muttered under her breath that she wasn't going back to that hellhole of a factory. The next day I asked them for the money that she'd earned so that I could take it to her. Eight bucks.

On Wednesday of that first week I learned that the administration had a policy of switching workers from one department to another without any warning, in accordance with the needs of the plant. They sent me to work under the direct supervision of *la paloma*. Four of us women worked in a row, standing in front of a moving belt. Because of how fast I'd been with the nail polish bottles, they put me at the front of the line. We had to assemble compacts, put them by the dozen into little boxes, and put these boxes into bigger ones. The rhythm of the other three workers depended on the speed of the one in my position, and the minimum production figure for that department was very high.

I put glue on one little powder compact and tried—unsuccessfully, thanks to how fast I had to do it—to put the brush back in the glue jar without letting any glue drip onto the belt. This is a tricky job, I thought. If I'm slow, they're going to fire me, and if I'm too fast, these women will hate me. I was equally afraid of losing the job and of being rejected by the other women. I comforted myself by thinking that I could hardly go very fast since trying to keep the brush from dripping slowed me down so much. In fact some glue always found its way onto the belt, my hands, and my uniform, so I had to spend a good while cleaning up.

After lunch *la paloma* came over to me. I smiled the way I'd learned to do as a girl when my father would fight with my mother and I thought it was my responsibility to calm him down. Though this usually worked for me as an adult too, I didn't know how it would go over right now. To appear even more pleasant, I slowly blinked my eyes as I smiled and tilted my head just a bit. *La paloma* counted the boxes. I knew we didn't have as many as we were supposed to. I kept on working without looking up, expecting insults and threats that we'd lose our jobs if we didn't go faster, the way the older employees said it happened when you got behind in the task. But that's not what happened. She stood beside me, gently put her hand on my shoulder, and instead of yelling she almost whispered, "Don't worry, it's all right." I never knew whether this gentleness had to do with my smile, but from then until I left the factory, life got easier for me and the other women working the belt.

Friday four men came in an armored car. They brought everybody's pay in cash. One of the men sat behind a dirty table and laid out the envelopes. I got in line to collect my pay. While I waited, I drank some juice and thought how this would be one more morning of not getting to go to the bathroom. When I got to the table I gave my name, signed on a list, and the man gave me the money. That had taken ten minutes, and I went back to work.

I'd been at the factory a month when one morning, after collecting my pay, I saw *la paloma* coming toward me with a bathing cap in her hand. "Unfortunately," she said as she handed it to me, "one of the workers in the talc bottling department has gotten sick, and since you're the newest in the factory, you have to replace her. I tried to prevent this, but these are the administration's rules and they have to be obeyed. You start the new job Monday. All in all, it's not a bad change. You'll earn ten cents more an hour, and as soon as there's a chance I'll bring you back here again." I asked her the name of the worker who had gotten sick. "Ramona," she said, and in my mind I saw the woman with the powder-covered eyebrows and the bathing cap on her head. For a second I thought of refusing to go, but I didn't do it. I was used to making the best of things, not to protesting out loud. I took the bathing cap, smiled at *la paloma*, and went on assembling compacts.

That was my last day working there. The next week I moved across the street to a factory that made transistors for radios.

Because of the acetone Adela had been sick that whole month and spent more than a hundred dollars on a doctor and medicine. She'd just started to be able to speak without it hurting her throat. I tried to persuade her to go with me again. "This is an electronics plant," I said, trying to sound convincing. "We won't have to fight chemicals or powder there. It's just assembling transistors. They say it's a little monotonous, but that's nothing compared to what we went through in the cosmetics factory. It's specialized work. Now we're going to learn something, you'll see. We'll work with microscopes."

After we talked it over awhile, she decided it wasn't a bad idea and she came along with me. On the way to work the first morning she even looked enthusiastic, but by the end of the day her enthusiasm was gone. Walking back to the subway, she said, "Look, you warned me that making these little pieces could be kind of monotonous. Now that I see what it is, I can tell you this job is so boring that some day I'm going to fall asleep after lunch, bang my head on the microscope, and lose an eye."

Two months after we started there, the boss—a muscular guy with blue eyes who strutted like a rooster—moved me to another department where the work was easier, with no microscopes. I knew he was attracted to me because he often found some excuse to stop by where I worked, just so that I'd smile at him. My first day in the new department he invited me out to dinner, trying to cash in on the promotion he'd given me. I didn't want to be on bad terms with him, but I did want to make my limits clear. It's one thing to adjust to situations as best you can. It's another thing to go against your principles. I turned down the invitation with a smile and told him it was hard to leave my kids and my husband at night.

He kept on dropping hints, and I kept on trying to fend him off without making him mad. The hardest thing to bear was the jokes he'd make within earshot of me. He'd show off his biceps and boast that he wasn't one of those guys with a lot of muscle and not much in the other department. He was ready to prove that any time, on any given day.

Despite all this, I tried to look on the bright side as long as I could. I turned a deaf ear to the boss, and when he looked me right in the eye after one of his jokes, I'd just smile nicely at him. At least the pay was a little better than in the other factory, and all the workers got a ten-pound turkey when Thanksgiving came around. The boss always gave me one of the bigger ones. Another advantage of working there was that we had a lunchroom where we could sit and drink *café con leche* and eat our bread and butter during the morning break. That was a precious moment for Adela, when she'd flip through the paper and report on the biggest news. Later—after we'd been there almost four years—she started complaining that she couldn't see the small type clearly, but I put that down to her need to complain all the time. She was only thirty. Nobody needed glasses at our age.

She was still working in the same department where she'd started out. Her marriage had gone from bad to worse and she really needed the money now. Though we heard rumors that in New Jersey—we never knew exactly where—they were paying $3.60 an hour for the same thing we did for $1.60, she never tried to change plants because it was quiet where we were and she didn't have to handle any chemicals. She felt secure, she said, because she wasn't risking going deaf or getting allergies.

One Sunday morning at the beginning of September, I noticed Adela was even having trouble reading the large letters in the paper. The eye doctor told her that her vision was highly deteriorated for someone so young, and gave her a prescription for reading glasses. She asked whether this could be because of spending eight hours a day looking into a microscope. "It might," the doctor said, "but I can't say for sure." In any case, he advised her, she shouldn't strain her eyes after work.

For a week I couldn't sleep. All the times I'd tried to ignore her when I heard her complain. How could it be true? And how could I help her now?

I started bringing the paper to lunch since she didn't buy it anymore, and I'd read her favorite sections out loud as if I were sharing something that particularly appealed to me. Sitting by my side, she'd listen and stare. At first I thought my pain over her trouble would ease with time. But the opposite was true, because she never got any better, only worse. Her eyes weren't what they used to be. Every day they had less gleam in them. Her penetrating look was getting vacant and weak. I tried not to look. One morning at break, after our *café con leche*, I told her she had to show the doctor's report to the boss and ask him for a change of departments, because she couldn't work with the microscope anymore.

She was afraid. I pushed her and promised my support. She had no choice, she couldn't go on deteriorating and not lift a finger to stop it. So she talked to the boss. He said he knew something was wrong with her because the quality of her work had noticeably declined in the past few months. Nonetheless he denied there was any connection between the job and her illness. He didn't see any reason to connect them. None of the other women had ever complained of this before.

Two weeks later Adela got notice she was being fired for inefficiency on the job. I couldn't believe it. There was just one week before Thanksgiving, and Christmas was just six weeks away. If she lost her job now, she'd get no free turkey, and she'd be in no mood to celebrate if I invited her and her son to celebrate with us. She was emotionally destroyed by the illness, and now this. And what about Christmas and the boy's presents? Where were they supposed to come from? By this point her husband had disappeared.

I went to the union, but the factory administration had already spoken with them. There was no basis to challenge the firing. There was no conclusive proof of a connection between her job and her condition. The transistors she was producing were unacceptable. She could appeal for workers' compensation, but the process would take a long time even if the decision went her way. Adela did have the right to collect unemployment, but the first check wouldn't come for weeks. The holidays were breathing down our necks.

I went to talk to the boss myself. I'd never done anything like that. What's interesting is that I didn't think twice about it. I went and explained Adela's situation. It was hard to do anything for me, he said, pacing slowly from one side of his office to the other, his sleeves rolled up to show his muscles. Adela's work was getting worse and worse, the factory lost money by having someone working with such poor sight. But couldn't they at least wait until January to fire her, I asked. He gave me a steady look and asked whether Adela and I were related, because we had the same eyes and I defended her so much. I kept repeating that she'd worked four years in the factory, that she'd been responsible and reliable, one of the most careful assemblers in the whole plant. That her illness wasn't her fault. At least wait until January, I said.

He narrowed his blue eyes and said we could discuss her case, but in a more comfortable atmosphere. Tomorrow night at an Italian restaurant, for instance. I accepted. I was obsessed with Adela's dismissal. At home I said I had to work overtime.

Sometimes I think it didn't really happen. But it did happen, because the day after that dinner they told Adela her employment had been extended. When she asked me whether I knew anything about it, I said no. I still tell her that I never understood what happened then.

The boss took me to a restaurant on a narrow street in Lower Manhattan. I've never been able to figure out where. A short waiter welcomed him as if they knew each other and led us to a private room decorated in leather and red velvet. It smelled old and of cigarette butts. There was a small sofa and the dim light of a glass chandelier with a single bulb. He ordered whiskey on the rocks, and within five minutes he was telling me stories about when he was a boy and the neighborhood where he lived with his five brothers and his mother, an immigrant and a widow, when they first came to this country. Since he was the oldest, he'd had to take care of the family.

Another drink livened him up for more stories. Not me. I listened to his endless confessions all through dinner as if I were paying great attention. In fact I was only thinking about getting him to promise to keep Adela on. The same waiter who'd first greeted us brought manicotti, veal, and a salad made with arugula, which I love, but I didn't eat much.

As soon as the plates were cleared, he got down to what he'd come for, but I wouldn't let him do it until he'd promise me. Until January, he said right away. After Christmas. He had the answer all ready. Drunk or sober, there was no way to get him to extend the time.

I undressed from the waist down, folding my skirt carefully. I didn't want to come out of this all disheveled. While he was clumsily taking off his jacket, tie, shirt, pants, underwear, and shoes, I was thinking that there was no guarantee he would keep his promise. He forgot to take off his socks. I lay down on my back on the little couch, with my arms at my sides. As he came close to me, I thought he looked awful. Apparently his exercises were only for his chest and arms. His skinny legs looked like they could barely hold the rest of his body up.

I let him do it, because that's what he'd come for, but he tried and tried and couldn't after all. I felt his saliva rolling down my neck. He moved from side to side and up and down, panting, without success. I thought I should have taken off my blouse, because he was drooling all over it and it was the kind you need to dry-clean. But the worst thing, the most horrible thing, about that night was that when he was lying on top of me in that useless struggle, his eyes were such a light blue that I could see my own disgusted face reflected in them. For years, whenever I remembered this incident, I saw that face. Finally he stopped, covered with sweat, his heart racing fast. I could hear it. I'm sure that's why he stopped.

He sat on the edge of the couch with his face in his hands. After a few minutes he started getting dressed without saying a thing. Then, before he left, he said he was trusting in my discretion. "Don't worry," I said. "I always keep my word when others keep theirs. Adela will stay on in the factory until she finds another job. Agreed?" He nodded without meeting my eyes and finished getting dressed. I put on my panties, girdle, pantyhose, and shoes, picked up my purse, and waited by the

door till he was ready. He went out first. I closed the door of
the private room and started after him toward the car, knowing that the boss would no longer feel anything for me.

My Thanksgiving turkey was the same as everyone else's.
Far from making me sad, it cheered me up. When Adela gave
notice five months later, I gave notice too.

She spent the summer months depressed, fading away in
another boring job, but at least her vision didn't get any worse.
I read constantly, out loud when we were together and silently
when I was alone: books on nutrition, diet, and vitamins. I
hadn't worked since I quit the transistor plant.

One night in the middle of October, I showed up at her
house with my kids and two large pizzas. My husband was in
Baltimore on a business trip. After the pizza I made hot chocolate for the children and coffee for the two of us. I told her
slowly and in the most melodious voice I could coax from my
throat that now I really had a good idea, that we'd be on the
right path from there on in.

She gave me a horrified look.

"Don't worry," I said, "no more factories. We're going to
pass the high school equivalency test, get into a special program for women I've found out about, and take ourselves to
college."

"Now you're definitely crazy. Go to college, with my eyes?"

"Listen to me, don't get upset. I've got it all planned out.
First, no matter how much you refuse to admit it, you're seeing better since you started on the sixteen ounces of carrot juice
and all those vitamins. Second, all we have to do is study the
same thing, and share classes. It won't be hard because we like
a lot of the same things. If sometime we want different things,
then we'll figure it out, girl. We have to be flexible and work
together if we want to get ahead."

She didn't answer, which meant she was giving in. I kept on
pushing.

"One thing you can be sure of. If I say I'm going to help you,
you know I'll do what I say. If I've been reading you the news-

paper for more than a year, just to entertain you, why would-
n't I read you the books for the classes we take if I know that
we'll really get something out of them?"

She looked down. She raised her head and two big tears fell
on the table. I wiped them up quickly with the napkin I'd used
for the pizza, leaving a grease stain where the tears had been.
I felt my heart breaking because even when her husband left
her, I hadn't seen her cry. I couldn't go on talking. I got up and
went looking for a kitchen sponge to wipe the grease off the
tabletop. Adela is very meticulous in her house.

It took work, but as I'd done in the past, I convinced her to
follow me. We graduated with completely different majors.
After a while we realized that our tastes weren't as similar as
we'd thought, but that was in our third year when Adela could
take care of herself. I graduated as a nutritionist while she
majored in literature, with her lousy eyes and all. What do you
think of that?

No, I never told him. What for? Why go looking for trouble?
The human soul is very complicated. I never thought of what I
did as infidelity, but he wouldn't understand. I wouldn't
dream of it. He's very good, but he's a typical Cuban husband.
Don't think I wouldn't have liked to tell him. I'd feel closer to
him if I could have explained to him what I never understood.
Why was I suddenly determined to study, when I never had
been before? It hurts to have to keep certain things to yourself
even when you'd rather not. I'd like to be able to share with my
husband my amazement about the way life works things out.
I owe so much of who I am today to that terrible experience.
Thanks to it, I learned that you can't take care of everything
with a pretty smile, even if my mother thought you could.

Little Poisons

H ow could I know I would react this way? It had been a long while since I had stopped loving him.

Of course, it was I who left the son of a bitch. He never would have left me. Of the two I was the more mature, understanding, serene, the sucker and the asshole.

That's why it felt like a jug of cold water was being poured over me when I saw on his desk the photos of that young thing he hooked up with the year after we broke up. I was upset. Yes, it was twelve months from the day—and after five years of therapy to free myself from my codependency—since I had told him we were done for good. He didn't believe me. He thought it was just another one of our fights, maybe a temporary separation like before, but I was sure this was final. I said it over and over again to the point of bursting: don't unload your neurosis on me; Don't get pissed with me, making me always the guilty one until proven innocent. Say I had a problem at work, what a hassle if I told him about it! And if I can't talk to him, what's the point in having a companion? Always, his first question was what had I done to get into trouble? Me, the most easygoing person in the entire company. For seven consecutive years I've won the company's Public Relations prize.

When I moved into the tiny bedroom, he had to accept my decision. Then, as he had done a thousand times before, he accused me of having provoked the fight to break up. It wasn't that way. What happened was that little by little I had been curing myself of my addiction to him. And when I heard him making jokes about some private memories of my childhood— memories that I had shared with no one except him—with two couples who were friends of ours, I thought, He's blasting holes right through our relationship. You know, relationships get colds, they develop allergies, sometimes pneumonia, and, well, depending on the disease, they are cured or not. He, with his ragged, warped sense of humor, killed ours off at point-blank range. There was no cure.

In reality, I had been trying to leave him for years, and finally I did it. Aside from therapy—from which I don't want to take anything away—I was helped immensely by a Patricia Evans book, *The Verbally Abusive Relationship: How to Recognize It and How to Respond*. By chance I found it at Barnes & Noble while looking for a book on bereavement, to console a colleague at work who had lost her husband. So I found this book that described the dynamics of abuse in relationships and the personality structures that exacerbate it. I'm going to be honest with you; at that moment I was still feeling sorry for him. Imagine how sick I was! I always felt sorry for *him*. That was the problem. And it's a problem that all women have who suffer from this addiction. The husband does whatever he feels like, and as soon as he suffers, or says he is suffering—God knows if it's true or not—your heart is crushed and you go back to the same old pattern. Living with that demon is difficult, says Patricia Evans, even for the person who has it inside. All I know is that for me it was hell. That last time I told him it was over, I knew it was for real.

As days and months went by, I began feeling proud of myself, strong, free from his subjugation and my neurosis, even when his romance with the young woman began and he told me about it. In our fifteen years of marriage he would tell me everything, even about his sexual escapades—if he couldn't share them with me, who would he share them with? Besides, that way no one could come running to me spreading rumors. In the end, he couldn't live without me: his wife, friend, lover, and mother. Can you believe that I listened to these stories and even felt proud of the trust he had in me? Anyway, since I never saw any proof of his romances and my life was boring, I even came to be entertained by the stories. Besides, his schedule never changed; he left the house in the morning and he always came back for dinner. Now I am wondering if he was making it all up. He was such a strange guy.

When he told me he was in love and mentioned her name, Fermina—something he'd never done before—I figured this meant he would not be coming back to me, and I felt good for the moment. But thinking it over, well, everything has a limit, and leaving photos of her naked where I could see them seemed a bit much to me; he was doing it to torment me. Even with this, had he left home quickly, nothing would have happened. But months came and went and I saw no signs he was moving out. Photos continued to pile up on the desk, and then the love notes appeared. Ridiculous and poorly written, they bugged the shit out of me. One would understand his wanting to stay on in the apartment if he didn't have any money and couldn't find another place. But he always had real good jobs, not only because he had a Ph.D. in chemistry but also because he was a poison specialist. Simply, it was really hard for him to make decisions. I was always the one who managed the practical aspects of our marriage.

Yes, I tell you, he was strange. Only his poisons entertained him. He would go on for days about each new one he studied. Then, on a trip to South America, he discovered that the tiny pistil of a certain flower contained a chemical so potent that two of them could annihilate a two-hundred-pound man without leaving a trace. Its effect on the human organism was similar to getting food poisoning from eating shellfish. He truly became obsessed. He bought a small expensive crystal perfume bottle and put some pistils in it, and kept it at the bottom of a drawer among his socks. I was the only one who knew where they were, and that's because I saw him putting them away, not because he told me. Tell me he wasn't crazy. He never wanted to reveal his discovery, and it could have made him rich.

It was a difficult situation for me. Since I was always the understanding one, I felt ridiculous telling him how much the ostentatious display of his relationship with the young woman bothered me. I didn't want him to interpret it as jealousy.

Things got worse. When we separated, we decided to sell the apartment, which belonged to both of us. Of course, the transaction required time and lots of effort, and as I've already told you, he was interested only in his poisons. It was all going to fall into my lap, I knew it. I insinuated that living under the same roof would feel uncomfortable. He made more money than me, so I suggested that he rent a small apartment temporarily. He refused. It was too much work to look for a place now and then to have to look for something more permanent later; he said I should move instead. If I hadn't taken charge, things would never have changed, such was his inertia. His relationship with the young woman hadn't made a difference. Apparently he felt satisfied with the life he was leading, seeing her from time to time, eating with her, and sleeping in the room next to mine. I needed to sell the place fast so that I could buy another with my half of the proceeds.

Everything was a mess. From the papers on his desk I found out that he was paying for the studio apartment where she now lived. He could have lived there; but for six months he didn't show the slightest inclination to do so. As time passed, my obsession grew. Instead of coming home from work to enjoy the tranquillity that I now feel, I would dedicate myself to looking at the photos and reading the letters on the desk. I scoured the drawers, searching for scraps of paper, receipts, movie or theater tickets. I bought a book written by a couple who had been photographic analysts for the CIA and studied it carefully. I took a course on handwriting analysis at the New York Open Center, and bought a high-powered magnifying glass to look at the photos. I was no longer content with just reading the letters that he left opened. I started going to my job at a quarter to nine so that I could leave work fifteen minutes earlier and give myself time when I got home to check the daily mail carefully. Meticulously, I opened any suspicious-looking letter, examined it with the magnifying glass if necessary, and sealed it again.

There was a hell of a battle raging within me, and no longer with him. While the clearer part of my mind led me to speak to Iris, my lawyer friend, so that I could finally get a divorce—she got in touch with the realtors to sell the apartment—my dark side would rummage through the corners of the house and in his clothes looking for things with which to torture myself.

Two weeks before Raúl died, Fermina started to call him on the phone—something she had not done before. In a tired voice, unexpected in a person in her twenties, she would leave messages on the machine asking him why he hadn't gone by the studio the previous evening; she had made him empanadas—his favorite food—and had sat waiting for him. That if she had upset him in some way, offended him without meaning to, to please forgive her. Please, please. Several times that first week and every single night during the second week, it was the same old song and dance. And he lost no sleep over this. Don't ask me why, I don't know.

At the end of the second week Fermina had begun to call past midnight. I was close to sleep when I would hear Raúl enter the apartment and head directly to the answering machine to hear the teary message of the night, taped an hour before. This went on for three nights. He would enter and go to the machine without even stopping to take off his jacket and tie.

Suddenly my heart gave a jump and I sat up in bed. I realized that not showing up for dinner with her, leaving her stranded with his favorite meal after probably having asked her to prepare it, not speaking to her for days, all these were signs of torture. This, together with his extreme interest in listening to his victim plead daily over the phone, all added up to his love for her. Terrified, I opened my eyes; he had stopped loving me. No wonder the previous weekend he'd taken the books on poisons off the living-room bookshelf and put them in a little pile on the bedroom floor; he was ready to take them away. He was leaving. I couldn't sleep. I saw the sun come up and the first little bird land on the feeder by the window. The thought gnawed at me. He was giving that other woman what had been mine for fifteen years: a twisted affection tangled with rage; it was the most legitimate thing he could give when he was able to give something from the bottom of his soul. That's what I felt—confessing it sears my soul—and it was the reason for everything that came afterward. How was it possible that another woman could be so important to him that he would do to her what he was only capable of doing to me? Me. I was an extension of him, indivisible from him, the person he hurt as if he were hurting himself.

Believe me, that was my saddest night. That jealousy was a thousand times worse than the one I felt knowing he shared kisses and caresses; it had been years since the bond that held us together was not love but fright. And look, you don't know me, but I'm the calmest person in the world, abnormally calm, says a girlfriend of mine.

The next day I got up and, as always, made coffee for myself. I went to his bedroom—he had just woken—and offered him some. He looked at me perplexed, because I never took coffee to him in bed, and he took it. When he went into the bathroom, I opened the closet and my suspicions were confirmed. Almost all the hangers were empty, and on the floor against the wall was an open suitcase filled with shirts and pants meticulously folded. I waited to hear the shower go on, opened the drawer halfway, grabbed the little bottle of perfume, uncorked it delicately and deposited into my palms the five tiny pistils it contained. Two little poisonous filaments would kill a 200-pound man, I remember Raúl saying to me. Since he weighed around 155, I put three in the coffee, to be on the safe side. They dissolved with the first teaspoonful of sugar. I put a second in; he liked his coffee real sweet.

Raúl was a great chemist, that's for sure. Shellfish food poisoning was the diagnostic. Since he had not eaten at home for a while, I had no way of knowing what could have produced the effect. I wasn't up on his eating habits. No inkling of suspicion. When the body was taken from the house, my relief bordered on happiness. I couldn't believe it, but I felt liberated. As my grandmother would have said, dead dogs don't bite.

But wouldn't you know it? There I was at my calmest in the funeral home that night, listening with resignation to the condolences offered by work colleagues and the wailing of the family, who brought chamomile teas to calm their nerves and who worried that I couldn't cry, when I saw a young girl with short hair and slightly slanted eyes come through the door. Immediately I knew it was Raúl's girlfriend. Her presence put me in a rage, rabid even, because in the end, as so often happens with me, I was angry at myself. Why should I care if she was there? Actually, rather than it bothering me that she wanted to see him one last time, it should have been worse for her that I was there mourning him. I really had nothing going with him for the last year and a half, well, not physically anyway. But emotionally, yes. The proof of that being what I was forced to do to him. I felt the urge to shove her out of the place, toss her out on her ass! But in my delicate situation, even though no one knew it, I couldn't allow myself to act out of character. Everyone knew me as Miss Politeness, and the last thing I needed was to let on that I was jealous. I swallowed, looked at the floor, and acted as if I hadn't noticed her presence. But what do you think she did? She came right up to me crying with her hair all in a mess.

"Ay, señora, ay, señora," she repeated.

I looked at her. Her eyes weren't as slanted as I thought when I first saw her at the door. She could barely open them, they were so swollen from crying. I felt sorry for her, I couldn't help it. Kneeling in front of me, she lay her head on my lap and began her lament.

"Can you imagine my misfortune, señora?"

She had arrived from Guatemala less than a year ago without papers and had found a job as a live-in domestic. When the lady of the house had learned about Raúl, she lost her job because she had been out too many nights. Raúl rented her a studio apartment, but he'd never stayed over.

That much I knew.

She never did understand him. Such a fine gentleman, so tender and, all of a sudden, during the last month, he had stopped talking to her; days would go by without her knowing what was happening. He wouldn't go over to eat, and all she'd been trying to do was find ways to please him.

I felt like recommending Patricia Evans to her, but I was sure she didn't speak English.

"Then, he disappeared for a week, señora, until this morning when a friend at work telephoned to tell me he had died of shellfish poisoning. It wasn't my fault, señora, he had not eaten with me for a week," she kept repeating.

I asked myself, Where had he spent those nights?

"And now, what am I going to do? Where will I live? I don't make enough money housecleaning to pay my own rent. I would have been better off staying in my country and being killed by the army or the rebels. What difference does it make? Where am I going to live now?" She repeated this last phrase, wailing, almost choking.

"With me, if you like," I offered.

She stopped crying.

"Would the señora do that for me?"

"Yes," I said, nodding my head. "The apartment is large and Raúl's room is empty."

Were Raúl alive, I would have had only half the money from the sale of the place, I thought without saying a word. Now it's all mine.

Soon I acquired the reputation of a saint. Shortly after the funeral I helped her move. That was three years ago, and Fermina is still with me. She is intelligent, clean, hardworking, and grateful. From the very first moment, she reminded me of myself when I was her age. I found a school for her where she could learn English, and helped her enroll at the university. I put her in touch with Iris, my lawyer friend, and she arranged for her to get her residency. In reality we have both helped each other out. When I started to empty Raúl's room for Fermina, I realized how lonely I would have been for him had this girl not been sharing the house with me.

For two years all was perfect. And then things got screwed up. Fermina fell in love. When she introduced him to me, immediately I realized she had chosen Raúl's exact likeness just by the way he treated her. After getting to know him better, much to my horror my hunch has been confirmed. This guy is going to beat her, if he hasn't done so already. The insults have grown astronomically in the year they have been going out. Fermina already reads English, and I've given her all my books on the topic—I have an entire library in the apartment, enough to get me a Ph.D.—but she doesn't read them. It's horrible. For three weeks now she's kept me awake at night. I see myself in her. I know what awaits her: years of putting up with a lot of shit before she realizes what's happening, and then more years before she can extricate herself from this mess, if she can—no one can be sure of that. And if she does manage to get out of it, only God knows how. I've learned that from experience.

Right now there's nothing to be done. What I tell her about myself she doesn't relate to. She thinks I'm exaggerating, that her situation is different. Everything will improve with time. The strength of her love will make it work. Poor thing, I know the pattern only too well. He does whatever he wants, then he returns and they patch things up without his having to explain a thing. He says he doesn't know why he did it, he couldn't help it, let bygones be bygones, that he's hopeless. She forgives him and it's off to a clean start. Poor thing. That's no life, and it won't change for years; who knows if she will be able to get out of it someday?

I've become obsessed and that's why I've come over to see you, not because I feel bad about what happened to her three years ago but because I want to see if after this talk my compulsion to settle this situation once and for all will go away. Alice Miller says that if an adult is tempted to commit incest with a child and speaks with a therapist about it, he won't end up doing it. I know you are not a therapist, and it's never crossed my mind to commit incest, but I'd like to see if this talk can exorcise my intentions.

This is what's going on. This morning I opened up the little perfume bottle where Raúl kept his pistils and I saw that there are two left.

No, that's not what I'm thinking. Listen, getting rid of this guy is not going to solve the problem. Sure, it would mean one less son of a bitch on the planet, but the world is full of them. The real problem is that women put up with them. It's Fermina who is breaking my heart. I know her. If this guy disappears, she will go out and find another one to abuse her. Do you think it's worth living like this, at best for a bunch of years, at worst all your life? If she marries and starts having kids, given how docile she is, forget it. It's all over. Or possibly, one of these guys will beat her to death. Or shoot her. Or stab her.

Anyway, this dingbat that she has snared weighs about 190 pounds, and there are only two pistils left; I'm not going to risk blowing it, because then they will initiate a full investigation. On the other hand, Fermina barely weighs 105. Too bad. She is so pretty.

The Most Forbidden of All

While I was crossing the park on my way here, I asked myself, How can I tell this story to somebody I've just met? So I'm going to pretend I'm talking with an old friend.

Next I think it's important to explain that I'm not here because I think that what I'm going to tell you is taboo in the sense that you've defined *forbidden*. I'd be a hypocrite if I said that, because it doesn't trouble my soul or keep me awake at night. I've lived through too much and seen other people live through too much more for me to be scandalized. Besides, I don't like guilt-ridden people. I've fully enjoyed the events in question and claim them as mine.

Ninety percent of my reason for being here is professional. The other ten percent has to do with the pleasure of finding an intelligent listener. I like to talk with people, and thanks to my work and some longstanding obsessions, I spend a lot of my time doing so with my characters and with myself.

I'm here for a specific professional purpose. I hope to draw out of this conversation my *own* story about this episode, and that's why I'm recording it. I want to speak without editing myself, without deciding whether what I'm saying is good or bad, correct or incorrect. What's important is to tell it all. I need to get some perspective before getting to work. I've never done anything like this before and I'm curious to see how it turns out.

My idea, or rather my need, is for you to listen from two angles: hearing the story so that you can re-create it, and also listening with a critical sensibility when I explain the aesthetic problems I anticipate in writing my own text and the ways I've imagined dealing with them. I want a record of how I perceived the situation at this time.

You can't imagine how much I've thought about each detail. I've been around a few years and I'm still amazed by life's inexhaustible capacity to surprise us, to piece together our destinies, to pick up what looks like a hopelessly loose thread from the past and use it to make just the right stitch in the present to change the future's design. I have so many examples from my own life. I'll give you one.

I was practically raised at the movies. It was the number-one form of entertainment for my mother and me. We went two or three nights a week, even if it meant I missed school the next day because I couldn't get up in time. She didn't care much about that. We almost always went to Hollywood movies, ones that starred any of the big names of the forties and fifties. Yes, I know I look younger, but I was born at the end of the Spanish Civil War.

Without fail, at some point in each and every one of those pictures, the camera would show us the actress in a long, pale, satin dressing gown, descending a marble staircase with a wide banister. Maybe they didn't always wear those satin robes, but that's how I remember them. They were all tall and thin—or looked that way—and they'd be about forty years old at that point in the plot. At the foot of the stairs waited a man, their first and only love whom they hadn't seen for a long time. They would exchange an intense look while she slowly descended the staircase, one step at a time, until she stood face-to-face with him. They would love each other just like before. All their sentiments would be intact, because nothing had managed to alter that impossible love. She was now married to another man, a rich one, whose adoration she repaid with a loyalty devoid of passion. Having walled up the great love of her life, her soul was closed to the possibility of any new passion. In serene luxury she overcame her deep sadness with elegance.

I saw the situation repeated so many times that this woman surrounded by romantic misfortunes and an exquisite environment became my ideal. I passed through adolescence yearning for her fate. Above all, what I found to be the epitome of cool was her disdain for love, her ability to control her emotions, especially back in those days when I was always out of control, always emotionally dependent on somebody else. When I analyze it now, my interior life wasn't dedicated to looking for love but to looking for a kind of disappointment that my subconscious saw as liberation from my enormous need for someone to care for me.

What I mean is that I went through many years of tangled affairs, but when I was almost fifty, about ten years older than the characters in the films, fed up with failed relationships and disillusioned to the nth degree by the last one, I stopped falling in love. Not deliberately. It just happened. And there I was at last, free of romantic attraction. But the unpredictable thing, which I never supposed as a child at the movies, is that it wasn't men in whom I'd finally be so disappointed. It was women. The majority of my romantic relationships have been with women, although men fascinated me in my youth.

My childhood was not typical at all. My parents were Spanish Republicans who lived in Andalucía until someone informed on my father and they shot him, soon after the end of the Civil War. Facing persecution, my mother had no choice but to board ship for Cuba, five months pregnant and never having given a moment's thought to living outside her native land. There's no point in repeating the calamities of her pregnancy. She would have been sleeping in the doorways of Havana if it weren't for a young *campesino* couple from Piloto, a little village in Pinar del Río. Recent arrivals themselves, they found her sitting in tears on the Paseo del Prado and they gave her shelter in the room they shared with their two little kids. Five people—then six—in a single room. They cooked on a coal stove in the common courtyard used by the ten families that lived in that place. The young man had built it himself out of zinc plates he'd lugged from the garbage bin of a factory nearby. The conditions of the bathroom were even worse. There was just one bathroom, right in the middle of the courtyard, shared by all.

It was hard for my mother. Really hard. In Spain she'd been poor, but she came from a small town where she'd had very little of everything except space. What she found really unbearable in Havana was the crowding. Day and night she cried and prayed to God. They told me about it when I was little that she'd repeat, inconsolably, "Please, Lord, free me from this martyrdom." As a result of this litany, Ismael and Adriana, the Cubans who took her in, called her "the martyr." She was just seventeen. She went through a difficult childbirth, I was born, days went by, and the poor thing wouldn't accept any of the names suggested to her. After two weeks of just calling me "the girl," one morning when she was sitting in the only chair, nursing me, she emphatically declared:

"Given the dreadful circumstances in which this child has come into the world, the only possible name for her is Martirio."

They tried to talk her out of it, to get her to think of the future. I'd grow up, and what Cuban man would marry a woman whose name meant "martyrdom"? She didn't care about any of that, she stated firmly. Martirio. That is what she called me and that's my name: Martirio Fuentes.

In fact my name never gave me any problems as far as finding boyfriends was concerned. My problem was that, both dreaming and wide awake, I was always in pursuit of some unique, impossible, and overwhelming love that would fulfill my destiny as a movie heroine. That search involved me with a raft of men, almost all of them married. I'd wind up frustrated and, on occasion, mixed up in some bad scenes you don't want to know about. The worst of them was when, at eighteen, I got pregnant. I got an abortion behind my mother's back, not because she would have been very shocked—she was very tolerant of both me and herself—but to keep her from suffering. She found out anyway, by the worst possible means. The guy's hysterical wife came to see her. In my defense, my mother said that the wife ought to understand I was hardly more than a girl and her husband was more at fault because he was too old to be behaving so outrageously. The woman shot back that she ought to remember the story about the old deaf lady who heard a hubbub in the street and asked what was going on. When they told the old lady it was a quarrel, she thought they said it was a girl. When they explained that no, it was a brawl, the old lady said, Well, if she's a broad she is hardly a girl. "Girls don't bounce in and out of fleabag hotels, sleeping with other women's husbands, the way your daughter does," the guy's wife shouted at the top of her lungs. The neighbors from the rest of the tenement were watching from the hallway that connected all of their rooms. My mother almost killed her, pulling out most of her hair—she had to wear a wig for over two months. But from then on the woman pursued me without mercy, even once brandishing a revolver to back up her threats. What holy hell that woman raised! The only reason I'm still alive is that my mother and I left the country in a rush on a voyage that happened by chance.

I emerged from each of these relationships emotionally destroyed—and I'm not exaggerating—yet never immune to falling in love again. On the contrary, even before the affair would be over for sure, already I couldn't eat or sleep because of my terror of finding myself alone. The only way I felt alive was to be entangled in some romance. My life was a real torture. What made the picture even worse is that I would always fall in love with men at least ten years older, instead of boys my own age. More than someone to sleep with, I was looking for someone to get up and drink coffee with in the morning, someone to go to the movies with and discuss the picture afterward, someone I could hug when I woke up and tell the dream that had terrified me before dawn. There were a lot of things I still didn't know about myself, but I did know that. As if all this weren't enough, having sex with these men produced a tension you can't believe, mainly because of the sound track those men turned on as soon I began to take off my clothes. It horrified me, although in truth it delighted me too. These sessions of sex with uninterrupted vocal accompaniment summoned up the most conflicting sensations, as you'll see.

Here's where I run into a problem with the story I'm planning to write. I've never written pornography; that's not my line of literary work. But for this story to function, it's essential that I, at least in part, reproduce the shamelessness of that dirty talk. If not, what good does it do to say that the sound track put in motion by the lover of the moment would provoke the most contradictory emotions in my protagonist? There's no way the reader will experience the impact of those feelings without having access to those rooms. Yet it's not easy to put on paper the way any one of those gentlemen, having just come in and taken off his jacket and tie would step over to where I, too, was busy getting undressed, and he'd unhook my brassiere and start in like this:

"Let me see them, *mami*, oh these sweet little candies that God put on your chest. And who could these candies be for? They're for your *papi* to eat right up, isn't that so? Say it to me, little lovely. Don't be a bad girl; don't get all quiet like last time, please. Talk to me now. Tell me you're giving them to me and to nobody else. Tell me I'm the only-wonly man who gets to enjoy these candies."

I'd be silent, mute, while he'd go on:

"Who's going to suck them all up into his mouth, you blessed thing? Who's going to coax out the last little drop of syrup they've got inside? Come on, *mami*, tell me, and don't torture me. Look how you've got me now. Just look." And opening his legs, he'd show me his swollen protuberance without any shame or modesty at all.

I'd look anywhere else in the room, any possible place but where the rules of the game said I should. And that was just the beginning. In bed they'd only be quiet when they had their mouth full of some part of my body.

The strangest thing about life is that you never know what's going to help you and what's going to hurt. Years later I realized that if it hadn't been for those encounters, I might not have become a writer. I didn't see it that way then, of course, but in those cheap hotel beds I conceived the idea of re-creating what I heard into written words. It was very strange. Think of my age and situation. Bubbling inside me were my curiosity, my desire for adventure, the half-digested mass of a thousand melodramas on the screen, my childhood shared only with my eternally melancholic mother, impervious to my pleas for affection, and her lover of the day. All this, on top of the sensuality of exuberant youth.

My dates with these men were always on Saturdays. I'd arrive anxious to learn the day's script, yet timid and scared too. As the key turned in locks of those doors, dirty from constant use, the color of those gray, pink, sunny, or cloudy days would disappear. Inside, there was one perpetual reality where January, May, August, and October lost all meaning, giving way to a sexuality built upon words. I think that without the narration there would have been neither erections nor orgasms. Touch functioned in support of words, not the other way around, or at least that was my impression. The many variations on a single theme amazed me. There were certain constants: "How delicious you are, tasty as can be, look how you've got me." They all repeated those phrases, but each man, in some way, had built up his personal repertory too. My problem was that I turned dialogues into monologues. An ideal exchange, once arrived at the stage of penetration, would have gone:

"All I'm putting into you is the tip, *mami*, just the tippy-tip.

I'm leaving the rest outside, just to make you suffer. Like this, just this much, that's all. Easy, *mami*, don't you move. I love you when you're such a desperate little thing."

And the guy would be quiet and hold still. Then I was supposed to answer:

"No, *papi*, please, all of it. I want your whole sweet thing inside me. Don't you see how I'm suffering? *Papi, papi*, please."

"But it'll hurt you, *mami*, you know what a tool I've got."

"It doesn't matter, *papi*, baby, I want it all, even if it ruins me. Put it in me, oh I need it now."

And here would come a torrent of obscenities that you probably know. Only I didn't answer, even though I quickly learned how my part of the script was supposed to go. I followed it, I even found it entertaining, but I didn't dare open my mouth to speak my lines. Partly this was out of shyness, but partly it was to maintain a distance so that I could see the kitsch and the comedy in the scene. In the middle of the action I'd be imagining myself seated at a desk, pen in hand, writing it down. Under those conditions, who's going to get turned on? I let them do almost everything they wanted, putting up resistance only when they tried to turn me over and put in behind what is more commonly put in the front. I did not allow that until years later, outside of Cuba.

The worst was a lover who stopped moving entirely, right in the middle of the show, for real. He was trying to control my orgasm, because he couldn't stand it if the woman got her pleasure before he did. He told me so afterward. His improvisation was aggressive:

"Not yet. It's going to be when I want it. You think you can do whatever you please. Not on your life. You're going to learn once and for all who's boss around here."

I didn't like his game because his action reaffirmed his monologue. With the others, actions and words went their separate ways. They would say, "I'm going to make you suffer till you beg me to sink it into you," while they were sinking it or at most holding off for a few seconds to increase the fun. But this guy, the one who refused to move, seemed to have learned to play in a military school. I lost all interest. It was such a tremendous effort for me to screw him, and then when he finished, he wanted to masturbate me, claiming with great pride that this was his skill. I thought, "What a shit." The second time he tried this, I stopped seeing him.

Of all the scripts, my favorite was that of a plantation owner who came all the way from Camagüey just to spend a few hours with me. He was a good deal older than I was, tall and gray-haired. He'd sit facing me, both of us naked on the bed, resting his hands on my thighs. Gradually he'd start spreading them apart while he said softly and slowly:

"Open up, *mami*, show your *papi* what you've got saved away for me between those little legs of yours. You know that it's mine even though you won't let me see it. Now let's see that little flower I'm going to eat right up, one itsy-bitsy taste at a time. That's the way. Oh, God, what a blessed thing that is. That's right. That's the way. I can't believe all this is just for me. You'll see you won't be sorry for giving it to me. You're going to like it like you've never liked it with anyone before. You'll never forget me, even if a hundred other men try to do for you what I'm doing right now. Nobody will do you like I do. Nobody will enjoy it the way I do. You're never going to like giving it to anybody the way you like giving it to me. That's a girl, that's my treasure. Holy heaven, come on…"

While I was opening my legs and sliding my body back against the pillows, he was gently putting his fingers inside me to the rhythm of his words. He'd take his fingers out and put his mouth where he'd had his hands, and afterward he'd lie on top of me and where he'd entered with his hands and tongue he'd enter with the rest. With him that slow game of substitutions made my orgasms easy and real. With the others, most of the time I faked it to get the matter over with and go home and eat the *arroz con pollo* I knew my mama would have cooked. She could make it so delicious. She went all out, with lots of olives and sweet red peppers. Because I liked it so much, she made it for dinner every Saturday and saved me a plate for Sunday lunch.

Despite raising me by herself, my mother managed marvelously thanks to her skill as a seamstress and the location of the building where we moved after leaving Ismael and Adriana. It was on the Calle Monserrate, right across from the high school, the Havana Institute. Like in our previous house, each renter had only one room, with a common bathroom off the hallway. But now we were on the fifth floor and had a tiny balcony overlooking the street that let in some breeze. At least there were only two of us in the room instead of six.

Though her sadness never left her, my mother was easygoing and good at making friends in spite of her tears. She cried for at least a little while on her best days and for a long time on her worst ones, but in between sighs she made sweets. She cooked *buñuelos*, the Cuban Easter pastries made of yucca, and flan from a recipe from her country that would make you smack your lips. If all she'd done was whimper, I don't think people would have grown attached to her the way they did. It was her combination of sadness and desserts that drew them like bees to the hive.

In the room next to us lived a Frenchwoman named Teresa, the madam of a brothel on Calle Obispo, who offered my mother work. My mother turned it down, but with gratitude, explaining that she was unsuited for that type of employment due to her habit of crying daily at unpredictable times. Teresa talked to her employees and got my mother some work taking care of some of the women's children at night. The kids slept, except for one who suffered from asthma, so my mother could generally get her rest at night and sew during the day. She was an excellent dressmaker and succeeded in gathering an enviable clientele. The best of these were the wives and mistresses of politicians, who spent lavishly on clothes.

We had no luxuries, but we ate regularly. I dressed better than many girls whose economic position was better than mine (thanks to the leftover fabric swiped from the customers and to the cheap dry goods stores on Calle Muralla), and we could even afford to pay the modest monthly tuition for me to attend the Centro Asturiano private school. Sometimes we lived alone, other times accompanied by some man who invariably left us, fleeing my mother's plaintive grief. I enjoyed an unusual degree of freedom for a Cuban girl of that time, partly out of my mother's constant dedication to her work and partly from her lack of the energy for keeping track of me. My girlfriends envied the fact that I could do whatever I wanted. I envied them because their mothers cared what they did, and because nobody turned up their noses at them. Whereas I felt the discrimination—sometimes veiled, sometimes quite open—which the parents of most of my classmates directed toward me on account of my behavior. I went to their houses to do homework, but none of them were allowed to come to mine and I was never invited to their birthday parties. That's how it was.

In November 1958, without giving it much consideration, my mother set sail for New York with me in tow. The poor thing was trying to lighten her perpetual depression, to get a brief vacation from the atmosphere of terror that the political situation had brought to Havana, and above all to free me from the fury of that wife whose husband had cheated on her. A Spanish sailor with whom my mother was going out got us third-class passages. He was always flat broke, so I don't know how he managed it. The nice thing is that my mother never knew either. Her idea was to get a change of scene for a few weeks, spend a peaceful Christmas in the snow, and go back at the beginning of the next year, 1959. That's how come we left our room as it was. Years later we learned that when the neighbors found out the landlord was planning to open it up, grab what was of value, and throw out the rest, they beat him to the punch. My mother liked hearing that.

When we got to New York, the sailor took us to the house of some friends where we were supposed to stay during our time in the city. A hotel was out of the question. They were Andalusians like my mother, from a village near hers, and to add to the coincidence, they were also seamstresses. As soon as they found out what kind of clientele she'd had in Havana, they wanted to get her an interview with the head of the factory where they worked. At first she thought this was foolishness, but they insisted. She immediately got offered a job as a pattern cutter. The pay seemed like a millionaire's and she thought I'd have a better future here (considering my reputation there), so we didn't return to Cuba even though she understood within a month that her wage didn't amount to anything in the U.S.

I was already eighteen—my birthday is November 14. I kept on studying and falling in love, but much more calmly and carefully than before. That last episode in Havana had made me cautious. Besides, here I was always busy, tired out from studying and working part-time. I don't know whether I ran out of energy before I got involved, or whether I really didn't have any interest after I tried a few times and discovered how much I missed that sexuality "filtered through the vocal cords," as Emilio Bejel, a poet friend of mine, says in one of his works.

In truth, this city's lifestyle was more accepting of two creatures like us than Havana's, women whose circumstances didn't let us fulfill the traditional requirements imposed on so-called "decent" women. Still, I missed the sea very much, and the smell of tropical rainy days. Those were the things I missed the most. At first we had a pretty hard time, but once my mother understood how the clothing industry worked, she perked up and began to make good money, so I never had to do without. I had my own room, and nobody cared what time we came in or went out. I worked, but more to keep busy than anything else.

I had a thousand different jobs before finding my path as a writer: cafeteria waitress, supermarket cashier, McDonald's burger flipper, you name it, but my favorite ones involved art. One of the most frequent and best paid was posing for art classes. One time I happened to pose together with a boy from southern India. His eyes, like those of the statues of his country's gods, showed me the exact meaning of "almond-shaped." Enormous in the center, they narrowed toward the sides until they ended in his temples. This sounds like an exaggeration, but that's how long they were. His slenderness, his narrow arms and shoulders, and a head maybe too big for his body made his proportions less than harmonious.

One Saturday we sat there nude facing each other for about six hours. By this time I had my own apartment. Living room, bedroom, bath, and kitchen, all tiny. A sixth-floor walkup on Mott Street near Chinatown, but I could bring anyone there without bothering my mother or worrying her. She had enough to do, handling her own love affairs. When the modeling session ended, we left together. It was March, one of the last winter days, with a cold rain coming down. The time we'd had to sit there undressed and close together had created a familiarity that didn't have to be stated for us to know. We'd observed each other slowly and without shame for hours while we'd posed. By the end of the session we knew where, on each other's body, there was a birthmark, light or dark. I had noticed the scar on the left cheek of his behind, and he'd noticed my congenital irregularity of having a rib higher up on one side. Out on the street we started talking. He said that he had no family responsibilities that weekend, and he looked me in the eye as if waiting for questions I didn't ask. As we passed a Thai restaurant, he suggested that we go in and eat. I enjoyed the food without worrying about his reference to family responsibilities. Three hours later we were in my apartment, in bed.

Shrinivas, that was his name, knew nothing about the verbal accompaniment that formed part of Cuban lovemaking, but he seemed to have studied the *Kama Sutra* without skipping a page. It was the first time I made love, the first time anyone made love to me. Making love. This expression came alive for me after that encounter. I can only compare it to understanding, through seeing a human being, the origin of the Indian idols' eyes.

His caresses were wise and exact. In the course of that night my joints were submitted to so many and such unusual movements that in the morning those which had gotten the most use felt dislocated. But I didn't complain. I had joyfully let myself be dislocated, and was prepared to practice until my joints were accustomed to such pleasurable toil.

Just before dawn, entwined, neither asleep nor awake, we calmly and slowly came to know each other's scents, the fragrances of our skin. Hands wandered in delight over bodies foreign until the day before, now but suddenly come to form almost a part of us. Then we made coffee. I've never been much of a sleeper, not even as a baby according to my mother, and Shrivinas wasn't either—an irreproachable quality, to my mind. People who sleep till noon keep me from sharing my enthusiasm for the break of day. We brought our cups of coffee back to bed, and I raised the blinds, hoping to see not the sun (which was absent that morning) but a few of the little birds that sometimes perched in the trees of the yard that my apartment overlooked. We had before us a scene out of a fairy tale. The night's rain, now frozen onto the bare branches, created a garden of translucent lace. It's impossible to translate into words the splendor of that sight. Some sensations can be appreciated only through the sense that corresponds to them, like the brilliance of those trees on Mott Street; you had to be there. The ice sheathed the branches so tightly and precisely that they seemed to have been dipped in a great vat of liquid diamonds and then returned to their trunks, embellished, the way candy apples are coated by being dipped into a syrupy pot.

As he faced that window, Shrivinas began to talk about himself in a voice that came from deep inside. His confessions captivated me. This was the beginning of making love for real. All the rest had been prologue. His capacity for intimacy was, for me, a thing unknown.

He talked. He talked about the dust on Bombay streets in the dry season, the smell of the fields in the rainy months, the trees and the details of the inner patio of his house. Holding me tightly, he spoke of the day his mother fetched him early from school and, crazed, pulled him by the hand through dusty streets to a narrow and rotting wooden door in a slum district, where she yelled until someone opened up. The two of them were plunged into a darkness of tight and foul-smelling hallways strewn with tiny rooms where naked bodies pressed together between unwashed sheets, bathed in sweat and secretions that were not all their own. In one of these rooms, through his tears and as he covered the shirt of his school uniform with an endless flow of vomit, he saw his father in one of those filthy beds, on a thin and sunken mattress, rocking on top of the twelve-year-old niece his father had brought from the countryside the year before, promising his sister that he'd bring the girl up as his own daughter together with Shrivinas and the other kids.

I named what had been unnamable until that day. My silent sobs when, as a girl at Christmastime, I so fiercely missed the presence of a father. My desolation when, at the age of six, I found my mother at the edge of death in the common bath. I spoke of my desperation, having to learn the meaning of the word *suicide* when it wasn't yet clear that her attempt had failed. Of my struggle—at an age when I was just learning to read and write—to memorize the doctor's instructions while he spoke to the neighbors. Of my covert vigilance as I tried to make sure the instructions were exactly carried out. Of the terror of knowing myself powerless, of realizing that no one would pay me any attention, that my mother's well-being was in the hands of people who knew nothing about our lives. Of being terrified that she would die.

Shrinivas told me about his dreams of transformations, always transformations. I told him my dreams of fish in the sea, of cardboard fish, of fish that tried to swim in the black-and-white tile floor of some bathroom, of golden fish that I squashed underfoot without meaning to.

He told me the details of the first time he went to bed with a woman, his shame when, naked with his would-be lover, he found that nothing was going to happen because his body didn't respond to her body's desires. I told him about my precocious Saturday dates in Havana hotels and recited some of the dialogues of those afternoons.

Our conversation blended with kisses. We cried tears of pity and sympathy for each other, and then, with our eyes still red from weeping, we gave ourselves over to making love again. These confessions diluted my defenses, and I think they did the same to his. I—no matter how much I pretended otherwise—always found it so hard to let myself go with another person. With Shrinivas I felt that I was his and he was mine, and I let him do to me whatever he wanted. He also gave himself to me. Our caresses grew hard enough to hurt. On my back, on my belly with him lying on top, I could feel him inside me and I entered him with my hands, which he accepted with pleasure. His immense gaze delighted in my nakedness, and I let go completely, imposing no conditions on the entry of his body in my body or his soul in my soul. Outside myself, in orgasms that seemed to last eternities, enormous red poppies blossomed in an instant before my closed eyes. That is not a metaphor. I saw those flowers each time I came, and I was happy.

It was a sweetness I'd never tasted before, and I wanted to hold on to it forever. Forever. But our meeting was no open door leading to happy days. It was more of a knothole presented to me by life, through which happiness could be glimpsed. I could see it. I did see it—distant and fleeting—but from then on I sought it, sure that it did exist.

By Sunday afternoon a window had opened inside me. Deep down there was a little girl with a tortured name, in great need of company, but real company, such as Shrivinas was giving me, such as he had bestowed on me in those two days. I didn't tell him this, because my confessions did not extend that far. Pleading for affection in the present made me more ashamed than baring the horrors of my past.

When I woke up Monday morning, he was already fully dressed, making coffee. He poured two cups and sat next to me in bed. When we were done, he set his cup on the night table, slowly stroked my cheeks with both his hands, and, looking me very seriously in the eyes, said he was leaving. His lover, another boy, was waiting for him. The other boy had been out of town for the weekend, which was why he'd been free of family responsibilities. I asked him whether he slept with women frequently. He said only when he found them very attractive, which flattered me. I asked whether he'd be back. He said no, which hurt me. And would he tell his lover? Yes. Would that make him mad? Maybe. Would he tell him what we talked about? No. Had he told him the story of his father and the twelve-year-old niece? Never. The last two answers consoled me a bit. Tracing my belly lightly with his fingertips, he told me, in the whisper of someone already far away, that I had velvet skin and the largest *yoni* he'd ever seen in his life.

He never came back to the drawing class. I sat in bed in front of the window, watching the crystal morning that was making me colder by the minute. When the door closed behind him I felt empty. I started shaking, my stomach ached, and I went to the bathroom with diarrhea. Back in bed I crawled under the blankets, covered my head, and slept ten hours. When I opened my eyes it was dark out. I looked at the clock: eight forty-five. What was Shrinivas doing? Embracing his lover, telling him he had slept with a girl? I had forgotten to ask him his companion's name. Then I remembered the dream I'd just had.

I'm sitting in a movie theater watching a film. On the screen appears a nude woman standing in the handsomely carved prow of a pirate ship. She jumps from the ship into green transparent water near a beach. I think, from the audience, that now the movie will show her swimming toward the sea floor and this will make me anxious, but as she sinks into the water, it's so beautiful, the rays of sunlight shining golden under the surface, that I forget my fear and admire the scene. Once she's in the water, the woman is transformed into a boy of about six. The boy swims down to the fine white sand of the bottom. It's all very bright because of the rays of sunlight, and there he finds a fish. It's dead, just the spine and the head are left intact. The boy swims close to it, puts his fingers in its head, pulls out the eyes and eats them.

I thought about the dream without understanding it. I spent hours going over it in my mind. It was late, so I fell asleep again, and Tuesday I woke up before six, with my energy renewed. Without understanding why this was so, I could tell it had to do with the dream and that depth of clean water into which the nude swimmer, turned into a boy, descended to eat the eyes of the fish. I couldn't interpret it very well, but that's where the little light shining within me was coming from.

I took a shower and phoned my mother—I spoke to her every day. Luckily she'd been away for the weekend. She was in love with a Turk, a professor of social science in a university somewhere upstate.

My affair with Shrivinas left me with a longing for intimacy and an intensity for words. The intensity frightened me, while, on the other hand, my efforts to control the longing wore me out. Conversations seemed so banal that I'd cut off relationships before they got to the point of going to bed.

One St. Patrick's Day night, the anniversary of my mother's suicide attempt, I walked into an East Village bar and met an Irishman ten years older than me, a veteran of the Korean War.

Though we never made any reference to the date, and though it had occurred before we came to this country, every March 17th my mother and I could read in each other's glances that tragic memory of which I never spoke until my day with Shrivinas. From then on I felt a need to talk about it. And I talked, mostly with women friends, only rarely with someone with whom I was going out.

Suddenly, there at the bar, between the noise of the television, the overlapping conversations, and the music on the jukebox, the half-drunk veteran began telling me his war stories in slow and horrific detail. His words fell on my soul like rain on earth parched from a long drought. Hypnotized, without missing a word, I downed two drinks and, tasting every syllable, told him about my mother. It was the first time I'd ever told anyone on the anniversary day. Tears soaked his face and, when I finished, he blew his nose two or three times. His cry-

ing was irresistible and dwarfed whatever defects I would
later find. I gave him my phone number. We kept on seeing
each other, and I made my need for sincere and honest dialogue as clear as I could. This was what hurt me most when
that marriage ended: how I had been so very clear with him
and he had willingly agreed. Or he'd pretended to be willing.
Four months from St. Patrick's Day we got married. We had
the wedding on the feast of the Virgin of Carmen, my mother's
birthday and saint's day, the saint for whom she was named.

Once we were married, his talkativeness waned little by little. Still, we always had two or three long talks over the course
of a week, and that was enough for me then. We led very busy
lives. What started to seriously bother me was not the quantity
of our conversation but the quality. I saw that he talked about
whatever he wanted to, while I talked about what he'd permit
me to—his censorship was subtle. I learned of all his previous
lovers, to the point where I knew each and every woman's
name. But when I tried to talk about my romances, he changed
the topic or somehow ended the conversation. At first I took it
for an accident, but it never failed. More than two years went
by like that, during which I was occupied with a lot of professional stress. I was working in a publishing house, which used
up a lot of my energy, and when I got married, thinking that
stability had now come to my life, I decided to devote the bulk
of my free time to writing, which became an escape valve for
my need to express myself. Yet I was always burdened with a
sense of dissatisfaction about the distribution of topics in my
husband's and my talks.

One Wednesday night, the third of April, I got home after
nine, especially worn out. We had supper, Mark popped open
a beer and so did I, and we sat on the couch facing the window
of our living room. There was a full moon, which is why I
remember the exact date and even the day of the week. The
huge moon shone through thin, fast-moving clouds, as transparent as if they'd been made of muslin. Later I found out
there'd been an eclipse that night. I didn't notice it then.

My weariness, the beer, and the mood made me want to be close to Mark, and with me, closeness starts with words, as you know by now. He, too, grew sentimental and talkative. When he finished one of his bedroom stories, filled with a wealth of details, we laughed together and for the first time I told him one of mine. As the story went on, his face registered more and more surprise. Without waiting for the end he grabbed his beer and stalked off, slamming the door. I was amazed, so I followed him, asking what was wrong. I found him getting undressed. His only answer was to get into bed without looking at me and put a pillow over his head.

Lying on the living-room couch, watching the moon through the window, I asked myself what kind of intimacy I had with someone unable to listen to my past. How could I feel close to someone who didn't know either what I'd done in my life or why?

If I couldn't speak from my innermost self, this marriage was headed for the rocks; I knew that, and I wanted to stop it from happening. He didn't open his mouth for three days, not even to say hello. I waited. As soon as he recovered his power of speech, at our first meal together, I charged in. I couldn't go any longer without defining the situation. After a conciliatory preamble about the need for communication within a couple, and in the softest tone of voice I could muster, I asked:

"What does intimacy mean in your book?"

Being no dummy, he'd obviously thought out his answer before the conversation began. It was quite precise. What he said was, more or less, "Sharing life with someone, physical affection, including sex of course. Enjoying what you have in common and accepting your differences. Most of all, for me, it's important to be able to be myself with that person, to feel that with her I'm free of all the masks I have to wear in the world outside. To be able to sit and watch TV with her beside me when I come home all worn out. Really, what I need most is her physical presence, often just quiet. Talking is important, of course, but it's not what I value most, even if I seem like such a conversationalist at first. In fact, sometime talking creates unnecessary problems, like the other day. That doesn't have to happen again. You don't have to know your partner's whole life. I know you had a few relationships before ours, but I'd rather not talk about them. Your past is past. What matters to me is the present. That's what we share."

This time I was the one who nearly lost my power of speech, out of indignation, but I didn't let it show. His explanation, apparently so logical and reasonable, was a total manipulation. I swallowed and spoke slowly. I was in agreement with much of what he'd said. To be intimate with someone, it was absolutely necessary to be able to be who one really is. The problem was that sometimes this implied that the other person had to stop being who they were. Physical contact was certainly fundamental for a couple, but the knot of intimacy was tied, to a large degree, by words.

And if the past was not so important to him, why did he speak about his own? He replied that the best thing would be to drop this fruitless discussion. Keeping on with it wouldn't get us anywhere. The best thing would be if, from now on, neither of us mentioned his or her romantic life from the time before we met. What was really important now was the two of us. Very well, I said, but our relationship was a mutual one. I had made this clear from the start, and he'd accepted. So, since I now knew his entire romantic life, since he'd taken the trouble to tell it to me a hundred times over, now he was going to listen to mine, which he'd never allowed me to finish telling, and then we'd start over with a clean slate. We'd leave the old tales behind us. And by the way, I appreciated his delicacy in saying that he knew I'd had "a few" experiences before him. In fact I'd had hundreds, I said, and I wasn't ashamed.

You can't imagine his face. I ignored it, and started to tell my stories. On the third sentence—exactly sentence number three—he stood up, went to the bedroom, and slammed the door again. I didn't bother to follow. The next day I went to see Iris, my lawyer friend, and that was that.

Right then, although without my being conscious of it at first, something inside me changed. I grew less and less romantically interested in men. I could see through their facades right from the start, and I wasn't disposed to put up with the flaws I found. At first I took this attitude for a transitory thing, as part of recovering from the divorce. Gradually my women friends became nearly my only recreation in good times and my only solace in bad times.

During a long Sunday breakfast in which one of these friends was telling me about a problem involving a separation from her girlfriend, I suddenly saw in a new way the splendor of her mouth painted red. I had noticed the beauty of those lips before, I'd even praised them, but now what I wanted to do was kiss them. I found the feeling more amusing than shocking, and I smiled inside. Hey, you never know all your hidden recesses, I thought.

Ada kept talking, and I kept checking her out. We were quite good friends, we went out together often, and she stayed in my apartment when she needed a place, especially after those fights with her lover. An irresistible desire to be close to her stole over me, along with the impression that she might be flirting. Maybe it was my imagination, I told myself, or maybe she'd done it before without my noticing. I started acting differently than I ever had with her, more self-consciously, paying attention to my gestures and words. The dynamic of our relation changed then and there, and by that morning's last cup of coffee, what I judged to be an illuminating thought had jelled in my mind: If I felt myself in good company with women, if I went shopping with them in Chinatown, went to the movies, the theater, shared recipes, lipstick, and confessions, why not add going to bed with them, and take care of the whole problem at once? Two women together and no fear of getting pregnant. I imagined a relationship free of all inhibitions, total enjoyment, absolute intimacy—an endless holiday.

What's interesting is that I'd known Ada for some time and glimpsed certain problems in her personality, but now I didn't probe farther nor let them worry me. They became a kind of backdrop to my perception, while in the foreground her mouth sparkled and our walks and conversations were wrapped in a rapturous glow.

Stretching across the little kitchen table, I kissed her. She responded with pleasure, saying she'd been waiting for some time.

She was my first female lover. Beyond the beauty of her mouth, she had lovely eyes, slightly bulging, which years later she learned to be the product of a thyroid condition. She would take her temperature three times a day and go for a blood test every two weeks, although every doctor she saw insisted she was all right.

With her I learned that the fear of pregnancy is a minor source of inhibitions in bed when compared to other fears. Ada's problems came from Catholic school, she said. She could never recover from certain internalized prohibitions, the most ludicrous of which was not to wear patent leather shoes because if a boy were to stare at them, he'd be able to see her panties reflected in their shiny tops. Given my upbringing, I couldn't believe how much her intimate behavior had been affected by religion. It was a discovery, my entry into a world of complicated dynamics previously unknown. She herself watered down the act of making love. Rather than doing it, she let it be done to her, only to emerge upset, removed, confused. And I, perplexed, would watch her jump out of bed and head right for the shower. Then she'd return to my side—her skin and hair immaculate—distant, silent, and irritable. Any reference to what had happened minutes earlier was taboo. You did not speak about that.

Getting her to talk was not easy. What she finally said was that she felt depersonalized after every time we made love, which I pressed for often while she accepted only once in while. She felt guilty about being with a woman even though she'd been attracted to them since she was a teenager and had never had any relations with men. That's what she mumbled when, under intense pressure, she allowed her thoughts to pass between her lips.

What I haven't told you is that, all of this notwithstanding, Ada was by profession a psychologist.

I understood and accepted her explanation—what else could I do?—but the situation itself did not improve. I learned the hard way that not all women are capable of the intimacy in word and deed. Based on my experience with female friends, I had assumed we were all gifted at this. On top of all that, she didn't like having many visitors, while I enjoy company very much. She suffered panic attacks and said that the masses of New Yorkers terrified her, like a great wave that threatened to swallow her up. When I asked how she could feel this way, given how often she'd visited me over the years and our constant outings to movies and plays, she pointed out that this had always been just the two of us, that she'd always turned down my invitations to do anything with a group. That was true. I decided that my encounters with her must have met a certain need, because otherwise I spent a lot of time surrounded by people, and that I'd felt flattered by her interest in doing things in private with me. Back then the situation was agreeable to the two of us; now it was a problem.

She started to get jealous, more and more intensely as time went by. I broke up with her one Saturday when I'd gone to study at the house of a friend from school—I was finishing my master's—and I got home, exhausted, at eleven at night. When I opened the door, she kicked it shut behind me and chased me through the apartment with the biggest kitchen knife we had, a stainless steel Sabatier that I'd saved up to buy years before, when I was living on Mott Street, because I can't stand cooking with knives that don't cut. She was so crazed that it made no difference if my friend was in love with a man, which she was.

In spite of everything I stayed with Ada six years and put up with more than I ever took from any man. With women, everything was even more tangled. Ada made my life impossible. I had hardly any of what I'd been looking for when the relationship began, but I'd found something that simply had-n't been in my plans. She cried on my shoulder every night. I was tied to her by an invisible chain forged from my old habit of consoling those who cry. In her pain I could recognize—and even worse, experience—my own. I stopped feeling my own sadness to identify with hers instead. In the end it was my mother's pain—which I never could comfort—that now allowed to offer affection without end, I had a chance to alle-viate. There was the possibility of giving her pleasure and making her happy, in spite of the obstacles I had to dodge to get to that point.

Romantic relationships with women cast me upon a sea of frightening emotional conflicts, but being a woman, I knew how to navigate it. The pattern was familiar. Feeling how beaten down Ada had been, I let her beat me down as much as she pleased.

Finally I toyed with the idea of going back to men. I could-n't. The reasons I felt attracted to women now were different from those I'd started with. Though I'd become convinced of how difficult these relationships were, I'd also acquired a taste for the softness of skin without hair, for warm and swelling breasts, for the shared dampness, for the pleasure offered by so many tender entrances. All this—plus the memory of the most beautiful, tender, and unexpected words that some women had graced me with—made me keep chasing them.

When I went to get a few things from the apartment where I'd been living with Ada, because I'd left with almost nothing, she asked me to come back to her. I replied that neither of us was happy with the situation, so the best thing was to end it.

"It's true," she answered. "But since you left, this isn't a home anymore. It's a hole full of things."

The greatest writer couldn't have come up with words as telling as that. I finished gathering my things as fast as I could, and with the greatest effort managed to get out before I was reduced to tears. I'm sure she doesn't remember those words, which I've never been able to forget.

There was another woman with whom I had some truly dreadful fights. She was a Leo and I'm a Scorpio, you know, and I'd say to her during these arguments that she wasn't really angry with me but at herself. During one of our separations she sent me a birthday card in which she said something so beautiful that I've still got it taped to my refrigerator, but folded over so that nobody can see what it says: "It's true that I have a lot of rage inside me, but I assure you that when this is over and everything calms down again, you'll always have a place in the small but safe region of my heart where the anger can never reach."

That relationship is one I remember with the greatest sadness, because even after the romance was over, and despite what we both wanted, our anger with each other never came to an end. Even today if we spend too long a time together— like if we go out for a meal—we end up arguing and then decide not to go through this again. Then suddenly we'll talk on the phone and decide to go out to eat. Scorpio and Leo, the two worst-tempered signs of the zodiac. What do you expect?

Another woman I lived with, one night without even lifting her head from the sink where she was making the salad, she started tossing lettuce through the open window in front of her, leaf by leaf, viciously tearing them from the head and not caring if they fell on anyone. Then she moved on to the tomatoes, still uncut, and threw them like baseballs. When I first met her, though, she seemed the most sensible person in the universe, with a doctorate in chemistry, well respected in her field.

What happened that night was that I got home from work, gave her a kiss, asked how her day had been, and told her that around midday, by pure chance, I'd run into an ex of mine and we'd had lunch. That was it. At dinner there was no salad, but I ate anyway, because I wasn't leaving myself open to this shit anymore. I moved out the next day, without giving her time to get her hooks into me. I'd been with her three months.

I've been with women who insisted they needed more than

one relationship at a time because just one wouldn't satisfy their needs. Just like men, exactly the same. I've had women who were every bit as controlling as Mark.

And so I went on like that, accepting the lurching of the ship on which I'd chosen to sail and trying to keep it afloat, until I arrived at a relationship I considered permanent. I put more dreams into this one, and saw more chance of it being long and happy too.

Deeply in love, Bettina and I moved to an old, sunny apartment in Brooklyn that we really loved, that had more windows than walls. You could watch the sunset from the kitchen and see the World Trade Center from the living room. We polished the old floor so that it shined and painted the gray kitchen white. We filled the place with lace curtains, partly to hide the rotten window frames. The only thing we couldn't hide was the crumbling ceiling, no matter how many coats of paint we applied. For me none of that work was anything new. I haven't mentioned this before, because it wasn't really relevant, but all my moves from house to house are another wellspring of stories. From lack of money and for love of living in a comfortable place, my pattern for many years was to get hold of half-ruined apartments and devote several long months to fixing them up. This one in Brooklyn, with Bettina, was the last of the line. Afterward things got better. My work started yielding returns and I bought a place in Manhattan already in good condition, although of course I adapted it to my taste.

And there I stayed. It's quite comfortable but even now, when I walk this city's sidewalks by night and through the grille of a fire escape I glimpse a curtained window framed by sooty brick and behind the curtain the faint glow of a low-watt bulb, it always draws me into a kind of a dream. For a minute or two I feel—because it's not a thought, it's a feeling—that this tiny nook of the city is shared by two people who think of it as home. Everything in there belongs to the two of them, not to one or the other; they hold off dinner until they can eat together and enjoy their weekends there. I mean, they're two people playing house. That's what I feel, even today, when my eyes take in an old apartment like that.

Well, Bettina and I were similar in many ways, and neither of us wanted it to end, but it did. That sentence, almost exactly like that, is what I wrote in my story about us. It ended being a chapter of my novel *Between a Tango and a Danzón*, which you know. I chose that title to give it a humorous twist, to keep the melodrama from becoming ridiculous.

Though we loved each other very much, our misunderstandings dug too deep a trench in between. One night, while she was out of town on a business trip, I was reading *Love in the Time of Cholera* in bed. Fascinated by one of the last paragraphs of the book, I wanted so much to read it to Bettina, but she wasn't there. I missed her fiercely. Just then a voice inside me said, If she were here, you still wouldn't have anybody to read it to, because she wouldn't be interested in listening to it. I felt something break inside me, right in the middle of my chest. I took a deep breath and read the paragraph out loud to myself. That's how precarious our situation had become.

When we separated, exhausted from trying to salvage the unsalvageable, I came to know the disillusionment of the leading ladies of my adolescence. Without my seeking or expecting it, I was introduced to a lack of taste for love. Luckily, I was by myself, without the rich husband who always accompanied my old movie heroines in their disillusion. I had no need to fake anything for anyone. I was suddenly possessed by a peace I'd never known before.

It was true peace. I knew in my heart, where you know true things, that my unease and emptiness when I wasn't with anyone, that my need to be in love—at war or at peace, but never alone—was not loneliness for this man nor for that woman but for myself. What I missed was my own center from which I had detached myself very early on to make room for my mother's pain. At one with myself at last, I felt something as close to happiness as I had ever known. I wrote more than before and turned to yoga, to meditation, going to an ashram on weekends, reading tirelessly about enlightened ones and how they had found that light. I sought out my spiritual growth with the same dedication I'd brought to every other search.

And seven years went by. Seven. I was living calmly, considering myself fortunate to have a past that was a nearly inexhaustible storehouse of stories, when I met her. It was one afternoon in an old store that sold both new and used books. It was just before Christmas, the big stores were jammed, and I was drawn into the shop on St. Mark's between avenues A and B by a special edition in the window, whose Victorian cover suggested it could be the ideal gift for my mother. I heard someone ask the salesperson in a Spanish accent for a Djuna Barnes book that I knew they didn't have because I'd asked for it recently and had to buy it somewhere else. When I saw her, I had one of those thoughts that zip through your head as fast as a shooting star, more a perception than a thought: She's Cuban. I think it was her way of looking me in the eyes without reserve. I told her in Spanish that she could probably find the book at a very good price at the Strand. She didn't know where that was, because she didn't live here, she said. I was going there anyway to look for some presents, so I offered to show her the way. She asked, Was it far? I told her it was only a few blocks. On the way I learned that this was her first time out alone in the city. I noticed that she limped a little on her left side.

She'd arrived in the United States a week ago, but in New York only that morning. Before that she'd been in Colorado, where her father had been living since 1980. The reason for her trip was to read one of her stories at a conference, which would begin in two days. She was very lucky, she said. She'd never dreamed of an invitation like this, not even having finished her university degree. But it just so happened that a professor from the college hosting the conference had been in Havana the summer before, doing research about Cuban women writers of the twenties, and they'd met just two days before this visitor would return to the U.S.; it was a Friday night and the woman was leaving on Sunday. She showed the professor some stories and never imagined she'd remember. There'd been no way even to give her a copy, because of the woman's hurry and the difficulty of getting anything photo-copied quickly over the weekend in Havana. But that's life. Here she stood, in spite of everything, thanks to a stranger and to her father's help. She hadn't seen her father since he'd left Cuba, but when he learned of the possibility of her trip, he offered to pay the fare—the college here didn't have any money, though they could arrange accommodations for her. So her father's offer seemed a miracle, given that he only called two or three times a year and had never helped support her while she was growing up.

That's why she'd gone to Denver, to spend a few days with him. A visit characterized by excessive friendliness on both sides and the mutual desire to avoid controversial topics. Only she was no good at that way of relating. She'd been raised to be spontaneous—too much so for some people's taste—so she spent the visit in inner turmoil, biting her tongue to keep from asking questions that, according to her mother's instructions, would be "indiscreet." She didn't generally obey her mother to such an extent, but she hadn't wanted to arrive in New York even more estranged from him than before. To judge from what she could glimpse of her father's current way of life, she suspected that asking him questions would lead to a certainty that was more wounding than doubt.

She left Colorado with a feeling of emptiness, unknown to her before. She'd come from Cuba with memories of a shared home, of bad times but also of very good ones. Her strongest memory was the pressure of her father's hand around hers as they crossed a street on their Sunday walk to her grandpar-ents' house. She thought this intimacy would come back as soon as they saw each other. This dream dashed, now she had to rethink how to establish a relationship with him that would be based on realistic terms. Later. She'd do that later. Since this would be a short trip, she wanted to take full advantage of it. She had to be home within a week. That was the condition imposed by her university's rector in return for granting her the exit visa. When the conference ended, she had to be back in class.

She walked slowly as she told me all this on our way to the Strand. I saw that she limped more than I'd realized at first. She was a good talker and I listened with pleasure. She had the joy in blabbing on, the delight in details, that people sometimes lose when they've been in this country for a long time. When she finished her story, I told her I, too, would be at that conference. I knew the professor involved, a good person, I'd seen her not long ago and she'd told me that when she was in Havana that summer a young girl had given her some excellent stories to read. So in fact we were going to be together, and what a small world it was. When I told her my name, she said she'd read two of my books. She gave me a knowing smile.

In the bookstore she picked up a recent biography of Djuna Barnes, spent a few minutes looking it over, and put it back. I asked whether she wasn't buying it. Too expensive. I said I didn't know Djuna Barnes was popular in Cuba. Not really, not with most people. But she was among a group of writers, all of them young. For her in particular Barnes had tremendous importance. From the very first thing she'd read of Barnes, she knew that she could write, that was how much she'd identified with the writer's style.

So I insisted on giving her the book as a present, and when she tried to refuse, I told her to accept it as a reminder of her first day in New York. She'd accept it only as a reminder of the day we met, she said. And thanking me, she looked at me in that way that had identified her as a Cuban. She asked whether we couldn't sit somewhere over a beer and talk more peacefully, if only for half an hour. I think I fell in love with her right then. The few blocks we'd walked had made her limp more pronounced. We went to a diner close to the Strand, on Broadway just past Twelfth.

She ordered a beer, and I ordered hot chocolate, which they make there with milk the way I like. Over two beers she told me the story of her life, which was pretty complicated for someone her age.

She'd lived alone with her mother since she was ten. Fights and reconciliation had been the daily routine for all the years of her parents' marriage. But when she got fed up for real and he found himself on the street with his clothes in hand, having to go live with one of his sisters and her husband and their three completely spoiled kids, he hopped a boat and left during all the nuttiness and confusion of Mariel.{*}

* In April 1980, the Cuban government announced that all Cubans who wished to leave Cuba were free to do so. The resulting mass exodus of Cubans came to be known as the Mariel boat lift, after the port from which the refugees left. Following the announcement, many Cuban Americans arrived in Havana to pick up their family members; thirty-two planes transporting more than 6,000 *marielitos* landed in Miami just days later. Eventually, more than 129,000 Cubans—among them many of the mentally ill, and criminals whom Fidel Castro had released from prison—would arrive in Florida. While thousands fled Cuba, the country simultaneously experienced huge manifestations of support for Castro and the revolution.

"A womanizer from the word 'go,' who made my mother suffer, poor woman, because she wasn't dumb. She always says she has a big defect in terms of satisfying a Cuban husband: She can't stand being cheated on. Even though he pretended to be doing all the guard duty and voluntary work imaginable, there was hell to pay at home. That's how their first years together went, and I owe my name to that. She got pregnant by mistake, but then she started to be excited about the pregnancy. When I was born, my presence was such a relief for her lonely nights. When people asked her how she could have decided to have a child in such a disastrous marriage, she used to say her daughter had fallen from heaven like a cool rain on her aching heart, and to please leave her be. It's a ridiculous image, that cool rain, and she's not so old really, but that's what she's like, I've never understood why. Can you believe that her favorite music, even now, is tangos and old-time songs from Spain? I don't know if

you remember who Conchita Piquer is. She's from my grandmother's time, but I grew up listening to her records. On one of
them there's a song that goes, 'Rocío, oh my Dewdrop, handful
of carnations, little bud that bloomed.' That's where she got my
name from, Rocío, and she pinned it on me in spite of all criti-
cism. She's still proud to say that in a time when most parents
were inventing new names for their children, some of them
unpronounceable, she gave me a name that was Spanish and
very traditional. With such a melodramatic mother I should
have been an actress. I tried it. I started studying acting and I
was doing well enough, but when the rheumatic arthritis hit
me, that ruined that.

"Since then, for the past four years, I've wanted to be a
writer. Where I feel the most pain is in my legs, especially my
left ankle, but it's pretty bad in my wrists too. See how my
right one is," she said, pulling back the sleeve of her sweater to
show the inflammation. It was true. "What's worse is that the
doctors say that if an effective cure can't be found, I'll be an
invalid in twenty years. I'm living on sedatives now."

She talked about her illness in the same tone with which she
told her parents' story. She lifted the glass of beer to her mouth
and then went on.

"Luckily my mother and I understand each other. Since my
father left, she's had some boyfriends, she's gone out with a lot
of men, but she's never brought one to live with us. She says
it's too crowded to stuff another person in there, and anyway
relationships don't last. She respects my life, although when I
grew up and started making my own decisions, she thought I
was kind of eccentric. Just because the first boy I really fell in
love with was a mulatto, a pretty dark one. Which is a sign of
absurd stubbornness on her part, since she's got Negro blood
through her paternal grandmother and she knows it too. You
almost can't see it, but she had her share of slights on that
account when she was a girl, as she's told me herself. What's
good is the trust we have between us. We talked it over, and
she reconsidered right away. Really, for me to go out with that
boy was for the best. Without knowing it, he smoothed the

way for what came later, and so when she noticed my interest in a girlfriend, it didn't surprise her so much. Sometimes I go out with women, not always. For me that's never been a bad thing. In fact I see it as something beautiful and good. Two stories with that theme were the ones your professor friend liked best. I'm going to read one of them."

Rocío told this whole story at one swoop. As you can guess, knowing my life as you do, I was amazed by the similarities. Even our names had the same origin, although her mother named her to reflect the consolation, while mine named me after the suffering. It was almost like seeing myself repeated, or reincarnated while I was still alive. I told her why I'm named Martirio, we laughed, and being close to her made me happy in a way I'd forgotten all about.

The tables, chairs, customers, even the lights started to fade. At the same time I was following her account, I was also thinking that the next day I'd buy her a really beautiful scarf in the store at Seventh Avenue and Eighth Street. In fact the most beautiful one they had. With my damned obsession about turning everything into literature, I started to wonder how I would explain what I was feeling when I came to write it. I wasn't even hearing the story any longer, just nodding every three or four sentences to give the impression of an attentive listener. It was a stabbing sensation, almost physical. Santa Teresa's "delicious pain" must have been something like that.

It scared me. You know how many really messy situations I've gotten myself into, but now I didn't want any more. I was finishing a book, and every time I'd started in on this kind of entanglement in the past, it had interrupted the book for a while. Now it would be different. I had years of yoga and spiritual practice behind me. I lived in harmony with myself.

I asked for the check, gave her my business card, and took down her phone number. I'd keep her company in the taxi to where she was staying in the West Village, then go home to the East Side and call her the next today to get together. As she put on her coat, she said she really could stay anywhere, she just had to call the house and tell them so.

"I think you'll be fine there, I know where it is," I said as if I hadn't caught her implication. "You're all unpacked, you've got your things arranged, and really that apartment is very close to mine."

Then I asked firmly, "How old are you, Rocío?" laying my cards on the table this time. The difference in our ages, so obvious it needed no clarification, had the authority of words piled upon it. That would expel any ill-fated ideas from her head and exorcise my desires.

"Twenty-four," she said.

"I'm fifty-four, exactly thirty years older. You could quite unexceptionably be taken for my daughter." I chose an adverb so old-fashioned that those thirty years might have gone by since it had last been used.

"But I'm not," she said, giving me that steady look.

During her stay in New York we were never apart except to sleep. Despite her bad leg, we walked a lot. I tried to show her the city at its most attractive: the lobby of the Chrysler Building, the view of the Empire State Building from Mott Street at dusk, the store windows fixed up for Christmas, Broadway by night in the theater district. I even took her to see a show, though they never seem good enough to me for what they cost. I showed her the most interesting things: the Asian pharmacies of Chinatown, the greasy *cuchifritos* of the Barrio, and the Lower East Side.

I was never alone with her. That wasn't hard, because we were at the conference three of the six days she was in town. I brought her to my apartment only when someone else came along. I didn't want any messes—"no messes" was my mantra. All week I couldn't sleep obsessed with that girl, but I never suggested that she try to stay for Christmas, even though I thought of it every time our eyes met.

The day after the conference ended—two days before she'd be leaving—it was one of those extraordinarily bright, sunny days that come during the winter, only this one, by some climatic whim or the effect of global warming, was very warm for December. About one in the afternoon María Luisa, who's my friend from that college, Rocío and I were in my apartment having coffee, waiting until it was time to go the airport. My Puerto Rican neighbor's laundry, fresh from the wash, hung on the line she'd attached to her fifth-floor fire escape. Suddenly she opened her window, to begin a scene that surprised me every time it occurred. With her sewing box in one hand and something that needed sewing in the other, she sat herself in the window in search of sun, her feet resting on the fire escape. Bundled up and wrapped in a heavy scarf, she sewed for a good half hour or more. Rocío followed her actions carefully but without comment until the woman finished her hemming, gathered in her legs, and went back inside. We finished our coffee and left for the film.

I took Rocío to the airport and after she'd checked her luggage I asked her what she'd liked the most about the city.

"Your neighbor, that Puerto Rican woman, sewing in the cold in search of sun. I'm going to use that in a story."

That was when, more than any other time, I had to rein myself in to keep from planting a kiss on her lips. Why couldn't this woman have been born twenty years earlier, or at least fifteen? I gave her a strong farewell hug, saying I'd see her in Cuba the summer coming up.

"Don't forget," she said. "I've been forgotten too many times."

My life didn't return to normal, but I felt proud of my maturity. I kept on meditating, going to the ashram, and doing my yoga, though I'd lost the certainty of recent years that my disillusion with romance was permanent.

She didn't write for five months, and I didn't either. I heard of her through other people. In May, while I was planning on going to Cuba in July, someone brought me a note and a curious knickknack from her, both of them in a little purse of purple cloth. The note ended, *When you come, we could see each other if you'd like. You know where I live. Kisses, Rocío.*

I got bogged down with work at the beginning of the summer but still managed to get to Havana in July, arriving on a Friday afternoon. Gladys, the friend I always stay with, was waiting for me at the airport. From Rancho Boyeros to her house in the center of Havana we talked with our usual abandon. Meanwhile I looked out the car window, and the same thing happened to me that always happens when I arrive there. I look at the sky, so incredible, the Cuban sky, and I hear swallows. "My God," I think in English, Cuban swallows, and all the grass to be seen is Cuban grass. It's crazy, but it happens every time and I've gotten used to it. Now, this time, those feelings of a recovered homeland awoke another feeling in me, a turbulent need for skin close to my own that I could draw into passions learned long ago in beds that rested on this land. I had a fierce longing for Rocío's freshly washed olive skin next to mine, and her slow leg over my own.

Suddenly I had a moment of *satori*. All that ashram, all that yoga, and meditation, was it all so that I could refuse to live? Spiritual growth should give life, not take it; help us find ourselves, not help us hide. What wisdom is there in ceasing to do all the old things we did, things that had a lot of good in them, to avoid the bad they contained? That's like throwing out the baby with the bath water, as the Americans say. Wisdom is in keeping on trying, and doing it better every time. At such a serious moment, guess whose voice I heard inside me, reminding me to think things through again. None other than Pedrito Rico, singing "Woman, Think Again." Then came the culmination.

Every human being born during the time span of my reproductive years, I thought again, could be my son or daughter, but I didn't gave birth to or raise any of them.

When I got to Gladys's house, I called Rocío's neighbor, because Rocío doesn't have a phone in her place. We could meet the next day, she said. Best to do it at her house. Her mother was in Santa Clara, on a trip for her work. The apartment would be ours.

I slept late, waking up around ten. Chitchat with Gladys's mother slowed me down, and I didn't get to Rocío's until almost two in the afternoon. I climbed a narrow staircase whose banister had been pulled off and never replaced, and I thought how hard it would be, with arthritis, to get up and down there.

Rocío let me in. It was a small apartment on the Malecón, its walls crying out for paint. The few pieces of furniture, minimal cooking utensils, and worn-out sheets all testified that it had been a long while since there had been any renovations. When the door closed behind me, I felt I'd entered one of those old Saturday afternoons that kept days, months, and colors outside, leaving the interior space to the voluptuousness of words. Except that this room had a window facing the sea, admitting a flood of light like there never had been in those rooms of forty years ago. My heart was overflowing and my tongue full of words I was no longer afraid to say.

Rocío approached me slowly, without blinking, and we kissed.

"I told my mother I was in love with you and needed the apartment for the weekend. Later we can rent a room in the house of a friend of mine."

"What did she say?"

"To do what I want, if it makes me happy. She says my arthritis is enough for me to bear. I told her how well we get along. She went out and found somebody to take her to her sister's in Santa Clara."

"I brought you two things that are supposed to really work for arthritis. Sea cucumber and glucosamine. Sea cucumbers are even advertised in Australia as a possible cure, though in the U.S. the company isn't allowed to make this claim. And people say the glucosamine can regenerate your cartilage."

"Later," she said as she took off the pale pink satin robe I'd given her in New York. The glow of that cloth on the bed accented the raggedness of the sheets on which we were about to make love.

Shameless and exuberant. I knew I loved her very much. From our first embrace I offered her my best: the words of the planter from Camagüey, Shrivinas's positions, Bettina's passion.

Seated face-to-face, our legs extended and entwined, I placed a hand on each of her thighs and slowly separated them while I spoke in a low, unhurried voice.

"Open up, my beauty. Show your *mami* what you've got saved away for me between those little legs of yours. You know that it's mine even though you won't let me see it. Now let's see that little flower I'm going to eat right up, one itsy-bitsy taste at a time.

She opened her legs, docile and damp, following along in the game, letting my hands enter her while she looked me in the eyes. Then she whispered, "Take a good look, my queen, I'm just the way you want me. Just for you alone, just for you to enjoy. Now you're going to offer me the same. Leave your fingers where they are and open up your legs. Let me take a good look at you now. You see how good I am to you, *mami*. That's how good you're going to be for me. Give it to me, *mami*. The same as I'm giving it to you."

I couldn't believe it. I was so surprised I almost stopped everything to tell her this was the first time I'd ever met any-one who knew all the lines of the script.

We kept on improvising until we were done, exhausted, in that unpainted room flooded by the sun of the Malecón. This was the perfect dialogue that I'd glimpsed forty years before but had never been sure of until this day.

That afternoon was three years ago. We're still at it today.

The Fifth River

Apart from intellectual reasons, I never thought that I would want to see you in order to tell a story from my own life, but that's what I have come here to tell you, my forbidden story. If someone had told me it would be so a year ago, I would have laughed at them—me, who actually gets paid to publicly analyze my own existence. I make my living organizing awareness workshops for women, but I focus my work on helping women to talk about themselves without shame, teaching them to feel pride in who they are and in the decisions they have made in their lives. I work with all different kinds of women, I receive offers from all over the country and abroad, but my specialty is Latin women. I feel completely at ease with them; I understand the things that they hide out of shame, out of fear of rejection, or because they believe that their feelings are of no interest to others. I try to sand down the jagged surfaces, the areas of our lives we do not fully reveal when we discuss them, the dark memories that we try to brighten as we recount them.

132

The sexuality workshops are the most popular and the most successful. I had suspended them for about six months, but I started them up again two weeks ago. The situation had become intolerable. As a result my income decreased substantially and the women's organizations that had been supporting me for years were alarmed. It was difficult for me to understand what was happening to me, and I didn't want to start the sessions up again until I felt that I was ready to talk about why I had suspended them in the first place, with the same honesty I demand in my classes. You must realize that in my work I always use my own example to illustrate how one can achieve happiness, material success, and live as one believes one should, tracing an existential trajectory that leads to total realization and harmony between thought, feelings, and actions.

Coherence. That is the word that has guided me, the common thread through ninety percent of my actions. Well, perhaps that's an exaggeration, but at least seventy percent for sure. The church priest in Piloto, the town in Pinar del Río where I grew up, used to say that seven transgressions of divine law, seven capital sins, are responsible for leading mortals to the netherworld for all eternity. Well, I believe that the first and worst defect that a human being can have is thinking and behaving in contradictory ways. What I have trouble accepting isn't the fall itself. There is no way to avoid slipping when life decides to put a banana peel in your path. But what I can't stand is not taking responsibility for what one has done, and believe me, in my own case, it has not been easy living up to these principles.

My mother explains it this way: She says that I've always tried to swim against the current. I don't see it quite the same way. I believe that every change I've gone through has been in order to live according to the ethics I believe in. I have tried to avoid being like those people who are unhappy, who constantly dream of something different, but who never make an effort to achieve whatever it is they want, people whose

dreams become diluted by excuses like "If I had been born
rich," "If I had had the opportunity to study medicine," "If I
had been a man." I grew up with this last sentence constantly
on my mother's tongue. As opposed to this inactive desire, I
have always believed in the real possibility of happiness. Happiness as I see it means taking control of your own life, as far
as that is possible. We can't control life and death, but each
time I've become aware of the roots of my unhappiness, I have
taken steps to change the situation, even if that has meant making a sharp turn, or even an illegal U-turn. After all, it is my
firm belief that the one face that I must be at peace with is the
one I see in the mirror every morning.

    I can remember the exact moment, the very instant, when I
glimpsed my life's purpose and began to move away from the
path that had been decided for me by the people around me. It
was a late afternoon just over fifteen years ago. I had sat down
to drink a cup of coffee at the kitchen table, after having under-
gone some medical tests. As I drank the coffee, unblinkingly, I
watched the sun as it set before my window—reduced to a
bare line—hoping to see the green flash that appears just
before the sun slips out of sight; someone once told me it
brings good luck. Each chance I had I would look west as the
sun set, hoping for it to appear. I never did see it because from
my apartment in Manhattan I could only see the sunset down
to the tops of the buildings. Then it would continue to sink
behind them and I would just sit there, waiting more for an
internal flash of light than an actual one in the sky. Staring at
the pink clouds, I would ask myself what I should wish for and
I couldn't say; I didn't know what it was. It was a troubling
feeling. There was something I wanted desperately—I was
sure of it—but according to everyone around me, I was happy.
I had no more money worries. I was married to a man who
adored me. I had a lovely and healthy daughter and an apartment near Central Park with lots of light and all furnished
according to my taste, whatever that was. I even had a sum-
merhouse by a lake in upstate New York.

But even so, for over a year I had been suffering from an exhaustion that kept me from being on my feet, especially at nightfall and on the weekends. During the day I had energy. At night, however, while I cooked and my husband waited for dinner watching the news, I would be overwhelmed by an exhaustion so strong that while I was waiting for the fish or the rice to be done, I had to sit at the kitchen table with my head between my hands and my eyes closed. I would wash the lettuce as I nodded off above the sink with the water running, even though I hate waste. My constant exhaustion spoiled our excursions on Jerry's two days of rest. We didn't know what do about it. My husband, who had fallen in love with me for my vitality, was beside himself. I had blood tests and my red blood count was normal. I took tests for Lyme disease, which was rampant in upstate New York; they were negative. We thought of chronic fatigue syndrome, but that possibility was discarded. Even my cholesterol was low, despite the fact that I had gained almost twenty pounds after the birth of my daughter. My mother and Jerry kept insisting that I have more and more specialized tests. To please them, I did as they asked. I don't know how many tests I took. For months I had tested every inch, every liquid and solid in my body. I began to pay closer attention to myself than ever before—I had always been too busy with the house and the baby and family matters. From my earliest childhood I had suffered from an excessive capacity for empathy. I'm over that now.

So I would spend hours lying on the bed or the sofa. This state of affairs, which seemed terrible on the surface, gave me the chance to think about myself. I began to suspect that perhaps the solution to my lethargy was not physical when I came to realize how much I enjoyed the little naps that I took during family gatherings. I would begin to nod off in the middle of a conversation and almost fall out of my chair; I would have to close my eyes for a moment to regain my composure. The only solution was to lie down for a while, even if it was in the middle of singing "Happy Birthday" for Jerry's father, which actually happened once. People would watch me with consternation as I wobbled off, but as soon as I went into the other room and closed the door, the cloud would lift. I would lie down all the same, in case someone came to check on me, but as I listened to the conversations on the other side of the door, without having to participate in them, I felt ecstatic. I was conflicted (even now it makes me anxious to remember the feeling) about why I was only strong when I was alone. This seemed to be the key.

At night Jerry would wash the dishes (his only chore) and then he would come sit back down in his chair in front of the television and wait for me to put our daughter to sleep so that he could tell me about his day at work. He had done this ever since we had been married, and I had long ago stopped listening to his stories, blinking often to keep from nodding off. But now, no matter how late I got up in the morning, or whether I took a nap in the afternoon, when I would lie down with Ana Gabriela to read her a bedtime story, poor thing, she would only get to hear a little bit of the story before I was fast asleep. Later Jerry would look in and, seeing that I was sleeping, he would go to bed resigned to another night without a captive audience.

It was the 24th of June. I remember because it was San Juan's Day. When I was a child in Cuba, a woman who would come to visit us from Baracoa would say that if you didn't take a bath on that day, you would get worms. Children are so impressionable that to this day I try to take two baths on that day. I came home from an interminable and pointless test for diabetes. When I finished the iced coffee with Irish cream I made to console myself after the disagreeable hours spent at the hospital, the sun was setting behind the buildings. As I got up to wash the cup, I remembered a dream I had had the night before, which I had forgotten in the morning.

I am sitting in a train traveling along the Hudson River, on my way back to Manhattan. My mother is sitting across from me; I can see her clearly. We are on the left side of the car and through the windows on the right-hand side I can see that the river is almost completely covered with lotus flowers, still shut but about to open. In awe, I point them out to my mother. She gets up from her seat, and the flowers are now completely open, huge, round, and pink. They cover the entire surface of the water. I say to my mother, "Look how beautiful they are." She stares out the window and says that she doesn't see anything there. It seems impossible; they are so large! Suddenly giant orange-colored irises rise in the midst of the lotus flowers. Again I point out this beautiful sight to my mother and again she sees nothing. I ask her to focus on the pink flowers. I look in her eyes; they reflect her resignation. And serenely she returns to her seat having seen nothing. I tell her that she has given up seeing and doing so many things in her life. "It's true," she says, "but my life has been difficult, and I've been unable to do anything about it." This is something I've heard her say countless times and in the dream I tell her that it isn't so. It is her fears that have paralyzed her and kept her from doing the things she wanted. Silently she assents.

I didn't analyze my dream. I simply remembered it as I washed the cup, but the clarity with which I could see the dead expression in my mother's eyes, incapable of surprise or delight, was more shocking than the sight of a green flash could ever be. I held my face in my hands and opened my eyes. I had not realized that they were closed. The water was still running, it was evening, Jerry was on his way home from the hospital, and my mother was about to arrive with my daughter. I had to cook something, so I stood up hesitantly, as if in slow motion, and put water on the stove to cook pasta.

I'm not happy, I said to myself, I'm not happy. That's the problem. Despite the fact that my mother gives thanks to God every day for my present good fortune, I'm unhappy. I thought this with my eyes open, staring at the lights being turned on all over the city—it was like the scene in a movie when the mystery is finally resolved. And you would not believe how surprised I was at my realization. It's not easy to admit that something perfect is perhaps not perfect for you. I finished preparing dinner with a quickness that I thought I was no longer capable of. I served dinner, put my daughter to bed, and returned to the living-room sofa. Jerry was nodding off as he watched the news. I sat down beside him, and he looked up at me in surprise.

"You're awake."

"Yes, and I want to talk to you about something."

"Okay, just wait till this is over and we'll talk."

For the first time since we had been married, I realized that each time I wanted to start a conversation Jerry was busy. We would begin talking only when he was ready. I was even more surprised this time. The mere fact that I was awake at that hour should have been like seeing me rise from the dead. He had been so insistent that I get to the bottom of my inertia, and now he couldn't pull himself away from a TV show where they were discussing, for the thousandth time, whether the president did or did not have a sexual relationship with that girl! I sat down beside him and waited for the news to end. During that wait I realized how difficult it was to speak of something that was so important to me, something that was not one of our daily subjects of conversation: our daughter, the house, our families.

The show was over, and I began to tell him about how I thought I knew what was wrong with me. He looked at me dully. Timidly I suggested that I thought I needed a change, that being home all day depressed me. Maybe I could take a class or look for a part-time job; our daughter was five and would begin going to school all day in the fall. Now he looked at me intently, as if I had gone crazy.

"You're not bored, you don't need work, you have enough to do with the baby. When she was born, we agreed that you would stay home until she was at least seven years old, that it was the best thing for her. What you need is rest, and so do I, now that I think of it. I'll ask for three days off next month, I'll combine them with a weekend and we can go away for five days. Think about where you'd like to go, and by the time we come back, you'll be a new woman."

"Don't you think it's strange that I should suddenly feel all this energy?"

"Not when you think of all the treatments you've been undergoing. The last set of pills must have worked, that's all, the ones you didn't want to take."

I never took a single one of those pills. We had different notions of how to keep healthy, and because he was a doctor, he always thought he was right. One of the few regular outings I enjoyed were some classes I was taking secretly in holistic health. I couldn't get out of the tests—my lack of energy justified his concern, and my mother agreed with everything he said—but I never took the medicine they kept prescribing despite the fact that they had no idea what was wrong with me; after all, I would be the one to suffer the side effects.

Jerry got up from the sofa, kissed me lightly on the lips, patted me on the head as distractedly as when he patted our cat, Torcuato, and, halfway to the bedroom, told me that I should get some sleep, that I must be very tired, that the baby was giving me a lot of work. I remembered a Buñuel film in which a couple tells the police that their daughter has disappeared; meanwhile the girl is standing right there in front of them, crying out to be seen.

Alone in the living room, I went to my private shelf of books, picked up a much-fingered paperback called *Magic Plants*, and looked up the lotus. According to Paracelsus, "from the religious point of view, the lotus has the same significance as the iris. Plant of the Sun." In H. P. Blavatsky's *Glossary of Theosophy* I read, "A plant with occult qualities, sacred in Egypt, India, and elsewhere. It is called the 'Son of the Universe', and it carries within it the image of the Mother. Planetary sign: Sun. Zodiac sign: Leo."

My mother and I were both born in August. Sitting on the sober-hued couch that Jerry had picked out (not at all in tune with my ornate, flowery tastes), I decided I would not go on any journey that would deepen my boredom and that I would have the courage to look at the lotuses and irises in any river. Yes, I would have the courage, but courage to do what?

The summer ended, and then the autumn. They were months of suffering, but at least it was an active suffering as I tried to find myself. I woke up one winter morning with the firm intention of doing something bold. And I did it despite the snow on the ground, almost by chance. Ever since my energy had returned, I had begun to visit my old neighborhood on the sly. Stopping in front of the dilapidated buildings, I read the graffiti on the doorways and looked up at the bright flowered curtains in the kitchen windows and the laundry hung out to dry on the fire escapes. I didn't tell my mother about it, much less Jerry, but I felt a joy that was difficult to explain as I stood before those laundry lines. I had spent my first years in this country there and, despite the fact that they had been our daily reality, my mother had turned her back on them.

I had long ago lost touch with my friends from the neighborhood, and the couples with whom Jerry and I socialized and whom we invited over for Thanksgiving and New Year's would have been appalled if I had told them about my attraction for that place. During one of those solitary walks I found an excellent spiritualist. Among other things she recommended some essences that were meant to open not my way, but my understanding. You see what a wise woman she was? If you don't know where you're going, what's the use of twenty-one straight roads to choose from? On the day that I awoke ready to take action, I went to an herbalist on Rivington Street and bought an essence of gardenia, prepared especially for Ganesh, the remover of obstacles. I chatted with the owner, a nice woman who gave her customers what they needed even if they didn't have the money to pay for it. When it was lunchtime, I went to a little restaurant that was painted red on the outside and ordered *mofongo con chicharrones*, mashed plantains with crackling, which I hadn't had for years, ever since I had started with holistic health.

I should mention something before I go on; it is difficult to fit all of this into an interview. Ever since the vision of the lotus flowers and the irises, I had felt terribly trapped. I tried to talk to Jerry about it, with no success. He responded to my anguish with his psychological crap, with answers based on his own emotional needs dressed up as science, using statistics that were derived who knows how. All I know is that I suffered because of his insensitivity to my needs. I can understand up to a point why he didn't take me seriously, but at that time I was incapable of controlling the insatiable desire that had replaced my constant fatigue. I wanted to find pleasure within the frame of my monogamy; I tried to satisfy myself with my husband, battling against his apathy despite the fact that passion was never his strongest suit. I did crazy things to turn him on. I went to Victoria's Secret and bought the most provocative nightie I could find in the store. I even bought some minimalist lace underwear, with a hole you know where. I was acting crazy, I know, but he didn't manage the situation well at all, if you consider his profession and his desire to keep me by his side. Out of that experience—seeing his lack of wisdom and realizing that people were making vital decisions based on his advice—I decided to become a counselor.

One day I went into a sex shop and bought a couple of things. I had never used anything like this before, and I was very excited as I brought my toys home. It makes me laugh now to think how disingenuous I was. That night I primped for the big occasion, preparing myself to drive him mad with desire. I went to bed before he did, covering myself in a smooth satin sheet. As I heard him come into the room, I pretended to be asleep. I waited for him to undress and then, before he put on his pajamas, I asked him to sit on the foot of the bed, across from me. I uncovered myself gradually and began to spread my legs slowly—just like I imagined the girls did in those peep shows on Forty-Second Street with the neon signs— and revealed a fluorescent, gelatinous, orange-colored penis, which I had inserted into myself in order to excite him

with my audacity. He jumped up off the bed with his eyes
practically popping out of their sockets, and stood there
screaming at me, mad not with desire but with surprise, jealousy, and who knows what else. I felt awful. He reacted as if
he had found me spread-eagled with a real penis inside of me.
It was just a game! He called me perverse, indecent. He said he
would never have expected such a thing from me. Without
answering him, I opened my legs even wider and removed the
orange dildo as I stared at him. I walked slowly toward the
bathroom carrying it by the tip; I could feel it jiggling as I
walked. I washed it in the sink and set it out to dry on the back
of the toilet. Each time I walked in there that night, which was
often because I couldn't sleep thinking of what a stupid psy-
chiatrist I had for a husband, I saw the innocent fluorescent
object just sitting there and it brought a smile to my face. By
my last trip to the bathroom the sun was rising and I had
decided to leave Jerry for being such a fool. That was the only
time in all our years of marriage that I had heard him raise his
voice, and it was to make a fuss about something that should
have made him laugh! If he had used that same energy to
respond to my desire rather than to get upset, what a good
time we might have had.

The very next day I ended up having sex with the cook at
the restaurant where I had the *mofongo con chicharrones*. The
way it happened was that I praised the food so highly that the
owner of the restaurant insisted that he wanted to introduce
me to the cook. He was proud of how he had taught a Mexican
to cook Puerto Rican food in just two months. He wasn't a bad
lover, but as soon as he was on top of me, I realized my mistake. I stared at the ceiling and wondered what I was doing
there. I left his friend's apartment, where he had taken me,
without having had the faintest hint of an orgasm and with the
knowledge that this was not what I was looking for either.

To make matters worse, I was still turned on and unsatis-
fied. That night I put on the lace panties with the hole in them,
which Jerry tolerated—this seemed to be his limit for sexual

adventurousness. I made love with him all the while thinking of the cook at the restaurant. As he penetrated me in my imagination, I had a powerful orgasm.

The most difficult thing was convincing Jerry that I really did want a divorce. According to him, I wasn't really feeling what I thought I was feeling; all I needed was a little rest. How much rest does a person need? I had to leave the house to convince him, and of course Ana Gabriela came with me. I left Torcuato behind because Jerry was very attached to him and because he shed a lot. I would be forced to stay at my mother's place and she couldn't stand the hair. She kept accusing me of abandoning my home. It was then that Iris came into my life. At that time she was just an acquaintance from the center for holistic health where I began to work when I left my husband. She was the only other Latina, and there was an immediate connection. It didn't take long for her to become my confidante. I don't know what would have happened to me if I hadn't met her. I was struggling to get things together financially and I had gone back to school, but the physical effort was nothing compared to the torture that awaited me every night when I came back to my parents' apartment. As soon as I walked in the door, my mother would start criticizing me for having left such a decent, good, upright man. She had adored Jerry from the start, first because he was a doctor and second (and I'm not sure of the order of these two things) because he was white. Her greatest fear was that she would have mulatto grandchildren. On the Lower East Side, where we had lived ever since we arrived in New York until I went to college and my parents bought an apartment on West End Avenue and Seventy-Second, all my friends and boyfriends had been dark-skinned. When Jerry came on the scene, she was in heaven. I met him through her. He was treating her for a depression that, according to my mother, was induced by menopause. I would take her to her appointment from time to time, and as soon as she suspected that he liked me, she convinced him to come over to the house. She played a big role in that marriage. I don't want to put the responsibility for my actions on her, but a mother's influence is so strong that it even extends to the things we reject. Do you know the poem by Lourdes Casal: "Mother / in the end you have succeeded / that my world be yours / that I define myself by contrast"? I am sorry for all of us, and I don't care if I sound like a soap opera, because I know full well that even if my mother has played a part in decisions that I regret, she has also done so in the decisions that have made me grow and go forward in life.

She was so happy that Ana Gabriela had turned out light-skinned; little does she know how lucky she was to have any grandchildren at all. If my attraction for women had come earlier, I wouldn't have had white babies or black ones, and I'm her only child. During the time I lived with her after my separation, every day I got home from work she never missed the chance to tell me again about all the sacrifices she had made to pay for a Catholic high school so that I wouldn't have to hang out with the teenagers on Avenue C. Of course I hung out with them anyway.

One night I came home too tired to listen to her rant, and we got into a fight; I took Ana Gabriela and left, without knowing where we would sleep. I called Iris from a public phone. Thanks to her and Rodolfo we didn't have to spend the night on the sidewalk somewhere. A few days later, by chance, an apartment in their building became available and they loaned me the money for the deposit and we moved in. That's where I met Mayté Perdomo, a good friend of Iris and Rodolfo's. Mayté was my first female lover and I was her second. She had had a brief relationship with a cousin visiting from Cuba, and when I met her, two years later, she was unsure of where to go from there. Without meaning to, I helped her decide. In a month's time we were caught up in a Juliet-and-Juliet-style romance, though a few months later it had gone from romantic to post-modern.

You laugh, but you'll see, that's really how it was.

We felt close to each other right away. It was friendship at first sight. One Friday night after dinner we got together to watch a film she had rented—we did this each Friday when Iris and Rodolfo took Ana Gabriela with them for the weekend. Ana and Raquelita loved being together. After the movie we started to share confidences, as we always did when we were together. We had developed an unusual intimacy from the start. That night Mayté, discussing a love scene in the movie we had just watched, said that she experienced desire differently when she was with a man than when she was with a woman. When she was with a woman, she desired things that would never even occur to her with a man.

"For example, if I were to make love to you right now, the only thing I would want to do is suck right here," and she ran the tips of her fingers lightly along the articulation between my upper and lower arm, "and here," and she ran the tips of her fingers along the curve of my leg that was closest to hers, as we reclined on the opposite ends of the sofa. "That's all I would do, and it would never occur to me to do that to a man."

I had never been with a woman, nor had I ever even considered it seriously, though I think now that my friendship with Iris could have eventually become a sexual attraction. Mayté gives off a very strong sensual energy. She is not exactly pretty, but there is something about her gaze, her gestures, and her voice. I wanted to feel her skin against mine and her mouth doing what she described. So I moved closer to her, pulled back the sleeve of my shirt and held out my arm.

"So do it."

She looked at me with an intensity that I had never before seen in her eyes. She took hold of my arm by the elbow, leaned toward me, and licked the spot she had indicated on my arm, slowly, with her open tongue, as if she were licking an ice cream. Then she sucked the moistened area. I closed my eyes, leaned into the back of the couch, and began to sink slowly into clear thick water, which sustained and relaxed me completely. I am telling you, it was out of this world. Wouldn't it be crazy to deny oneself such pleasure? When she let go of my arm, I took off my shirt and, naked to the waist (I never use a bra at home), I held out the other arm, on which the same caress and pleasure were repeated. As she let go of my arm, I couldn't avoid thinking of Dracula because of the mark she had left there. I had to wear long sleeves for two weeks after that. I loosened the drawstring of my pants and lay down facedown on the couch to facilitate the operation on the curve of my legs, which she undertook with the same slowness as on my arms. Then, with her open hand she caressed the back of my right leg from the heel to the beginning of my thigh, and inserted her hand between my legs where it was wet from the excitement. I could feel her fingers inside me, from behind. She leaned over my back and whispered, "I love you, Catalina."

And in an instant that "I love you" brought on a powerful orgasm.

I was so overwhelmed by events in my life and so in need of affection that at first her love was a comfort—that was before the neuroses. At first the neuroses were indistinguishable from the comfort because they came from the same trauma. Even so, we lasted more than two years together. With her I truly learned how to make love. Because there is no " love weapon," as the penis is sometimes referred to in Oriental sex manuals, the sexual act between two women must of necessity become an art form in order to satisfy both participants. When I met Mayté, she fit my needs exactly. Her free spirit led us to explore every sexual toy we could find in the sex shops in the Village. It was exciting, after long days of work and studies, to spend our nights exploring new sexual techniques—we preferred vibrators to dildos. With her I learned many things that have helped me in my workshops. We had a relationship that I would never recommend to my clients; in fact I use it as an example of an addiction to a person and how to overcome it. The truth is I found great pleasure in it. I also say this in my classes, with all honesty. That's one of the reasons why I suspended my workshops for several months. How could I explain that I was seeing her again?

We argued constantly, mostly about stupid things. But behind the nonsense there was a real issue: the search for a balance of power in the relationship, which we never achieved. It isn't easy. Just as in matters of sex, the emotional relationship between women requires a high level of mastery; a dynamic must be created for which there are no models. I know this has been said before and analyzed at length, nonetheless it's a reality. In my work I have seen that in most couples, after a certain amount of time, romantic feelings acquire a filial quality, which makes sexual desire seem incestuous and kills passion. Sometimes the couple can stay together for years or even forever, but in those cases they have either resigned themselves to living without sex or they engage in sexual relationships outside of the couple. This is the classic model of a traditional marriage. With Mayté it was different. We were both too strong, that's what I think. We loved each other and above all we enjoyed each other with a vehemence that would never have accepted sacrificing pleasure. So our relationship evolved in an unexpected manner.

One Saturday afternoon after a terrible fight that emptied us of insults and destroyed all reserve and the anger had dissipated, we became embroiled in a fierce reconciliation, more like a wrestling match than an act of lovemaking. We emerged so satisfied that we could not wait for the next round. From then on, struggle and excitement became signifier and signified for us—they were one and the same. We invented extravagant games, positions unique to each session. Mayté's body merged with mine and mine with hers, there wasn't an inch of skin that had not been explored by our tongues, no burrow that had not been probed by the other's hands. Our combined scents in the sheets excited us, our mouths seemed to be glued to each other's groins, and, losing all track of time, it always seemed too soon to let go. We were so aroused by the scent that we decided not to bathe on the weekends and we stopped going to the movies, seeing friends, and going out to restaurants. We reached such an extreme that if we argued in the morning before work, we would call to warn the other not to take a bath before we saw each other that evening.

As the lovemaking became more intense, so did the fights and my possessive feelings. I went to an extreme. That December I wrote all of the Christmas cards to our mutual friends and signed them, and then asked Mayté to sign them as well. She was furious and I couldn't understand why. I honestly thought I had done it to save her the trouble. Why did we both have to write if I could do it all myself? I was irritated by her job, the long days she put in at the newspaper, the irregular hours, the nights she came home late, and the frequent meetings. We would fight, make love, and fight again. When Mayté didn't let me record the message on her answering machine, that was the last straw. She insisted that it was her machine and that I must be out of my mind. So I decided we should move in together. In my mind that was the solution to all our problems. One telephone, one answering machine, and one message with my voice on it. That was really "taunting the monkey," like my father would have said. Until then I had only been yanking at the monkey's chain, but asking her to give up the apartment, which she was so attached to, which she had refused to give up to go to Chicago with Alberto, was going too far. She broke up with me for real this time. We had broken up many times before, and we had always gotten back together, but this time she didn't come back; we didn't make love again.

She said I didn't love her. How could I say I loved her if I didn't understand her needs? How could I object to her work, which was such an integral part of her life, and how could I even suggest that she leave her apartment after she had already told me about what happened with Alberto? I didn't love her. I simply wanted to control her. I don't know, I'm sure she was right from her point of view, but I felt like I had lost an arm or a leg. I was crushed by the breakup and I cried for a long time. I decided to try not to forget her. I didn't want to because I loved her so much in my own way, though she didn't believe it.

For weeks I drank my morning coffee sitting in the same

chair where I had sat when Mayté slept over, and I imagined my conversations with her. We talked about life, destiny, human relations, and society. I talked to her as if she had been there to answer me. While I maintained this ritual, I could spend hours without feeling her absence. One morning, however, I distractedly sat in another spot and the spell was broken. That's how it happened. My invented reality began to grow more faint and I kept trying, unsuccessfully, to bring it back to life, trying to re-create the exact expression on her face when she reacted to something I said. Each time the image was more diffuse. I began to get up and go to sleep at the same times I had before knowing her, to watch the TV programs that she couldn't stand. My mealtimes went back to what they were before Mayté, when I didn't have to wait for the next day's paper to close before cooking dinner, knowing that she would be there in half an hour after Ana Gabriela had already gone to bed. I went back to my old routine and was filled with the most terrible pain I have ever felt. That is when I realized that we were really over. And all of this happened without her knowledge. I was proud, and when I realized it was over, I picked up my nightgown and my electric toothbrush from her apartment, packed up my vitamins in a bag, crossed the hallway quietly, and suffered silently—very silently, so that Ana Gabriela wouldn't know.

Again Iris came to the rescue. She knew the details of my relationship with Mayté, and because strange stories seem to follow me around and because of my apparent openness about my own life, she felt encouraged to tell me a very strange story of her own. Actually it was about her husband, something she had not even told Mayté. If I'm telling you now, even all these years later, it's because your discretion has been put to the test by the many confessions you have heard and never revealed or even suggested to anyone.

Iris's husband is a decent, serious, tender man, as you know. She has never had even the slightest suspicion of infidelity on his part. One day they went to the movies with Raquelita, and on the way out of the theater he felt like having a drink because the popcorn had made him thirsty. Because he was holding Raquelita asleep in his arms, he asked Iris to take three dollars from his wallet, which he had in the back pocket of his trousers. It was one of those wallets with several pockets, and when she opened one of them, instead of finding money she found an unwrapped condom that looked as if it had been used. She took the three dollars out of another pocket without mentioning it, wondering if she had seen correctly. He noticed nothing, but it was all she could think about on the way home. As soon as she had the opportunity, she looked again, and in fact Rodolfo kept and still keeps in his wallet a condom that has apparently been used and washed. Because it is so unlike her husband, because he is a man with certain peculiarities (caused by the trauma of his exile to this country) and because she thinks that the condom has nothing to do with another woman (she even suspects a gay encounter), she has never mentioned it to him or to anyone. But on that day she told me about it. She said that it was so unique that someone should inspire such confidence that she could talk about something so intimate, that I should consider becoming a therapist. What I never told Iris was that on two occasions, when she was away visiting her mother in New Jersey with Raquelita and Ana Gabriela, I saw Rodolfo go into the apartment across from theirs where a woman with a lovely face and a deep, musical voice lived. She must have weighed about four hundred pounds. Her name was Frances. I would spend Friday nights with Mayté, and late on the following morning I would head home. That was when I saw Rodolfo. The first time he looked so uncomfortable when he saw me that the second time I tried to pretend I hadn't seen him—my apartment was at the other end of the hall. I had never understood why he had behaved in that way. The woman was not a friend of theirs, but after Iris told me the story of the condom, I sensed that this was the most likely explanation. Frances moved out of the building over three years ago. Who knows?

Iris's professional advice came at the right time. I was finishing a masters' in psychology, but without much enthusiasm. When she suggested that I devote myself full-time to therapy, I was trying to sort out my own internal mess, going to therapy, trying to understand my own behavior during my relationship with Mayté. How could I have acted and felt the way I did, especially after what I had gone through with Jerry and his desire to control me? That was when I had the idea of organizing my first workshop to discuss with a group of women whether any of them had had similar experiences, and try to figure out a way to avoid falling into that trap again.

I decided that my next relationship would be emotionally healthy, or else that I would remain single. I believe in taking radical steps. To illustrate to you my determination to do what I want and not do what I don't, I'll tell you a story from when I was a little girl. I used a pacifier until my third birthday. I'll never forget how, during my birthday party, my mother told my aunt Fanita that she had no idea what to do to make me lose this habit, that my teeth would be ruined if I didn't stop. I didn't want anyone to know that I still used a pacifier and I only did it when there was no one around, not even my aunt or my grandmother. I felt that my mother had betrayed me. Later that night, when she brought me my pacifier—I couldn't fall asleep without it—I threw it on the floor. I never used it again. It became a sort of family joke; they would offer me the pacifier just to tempt me. Can you believe how cruel of them? But I didn't give in. Never again. So it was a complete shock for someone with my personality to discover the total lack of control and the possessiveness that I had shown in my relationship with Mayté. That experience marked the way to my professional success.

After Mayté I had several brief relationships, always with women, until I met Melissa in one of the Weight Watchers classes I was giving. I had actually lost my excess twenty pounds without following any special diets, but they paid well and it didn't hurt anyone for me to say that I had lost weight on the program. After six months Melissa hadn't lost any weight and she left the class, but that's when our relationship began. It was sensible from the start. She was two years older than I was and, like me, she loved the movies. She had been married and she had two boys, so it was perfect. Ana Gabriela was the daughter she had never had, and Roger and Francis were like my sons. She is an architect and works in urban development in a large firm. Despite the recession, in the last few years her field has been flourishing with the process of gentrification of Manhattan. This is the only subject on which we disagreed completely. For me, from the point of view of the Latino community, it is difficult to accept what is happening to the city. For her, from the point of view of urban development, it is a positive trend. But despite these differences, we treated each other with mutual respect and it was a relationship that I was proud of for years. It was normal, as I would say, and I could use it as an example for all the women in my workshops. But I guess normal is just not right for me.

Months before what I'm about to tell you happened, something seemingly insignificant took place that I thought about for several days. When Melissa and I had just begun seeing each other, Mayté and I made an effort to reestablish our friendship. It was impossible not to see each other anyway, since so many things connect us: Ana Gabriela's fondness for her, our common friendship with Iris and Rodolfo, Raquelita, and Cuba. Mayté was already with someone else; she introduced us, and I introduced her to Melissa, and since then the four of us have gone out frequently and sustained a relationship that I would categorize as friendly but not intimate.

On one occasion Melissa traveled to Poland to give some conferences about the success they had had in New York in reviving and beautifying the city, as she would say. To me it was about kicking people out of their apartments. Michelle, Mayté's girlfriend, had also gone to visit her parents in Nevada. I invited Mayté, Iris, Rodolfo and Raquelita out to my house in Westchester for the weekend. It was October, with that incredible late-afternoon light and the stunning way it colors the leaves on the trees. On Saturday, after lunch, Mayté and

I decided to go for a walk near the house and I began picking up leaves of different colors and shapes to give to Melissa when she returned two weeks later. She loves the outdoors, more than I do, and she was missing her favorite time of year. Mayté began to help me, picking the leaves with the brightest, most varied colors and that were in the best condition—most of them were imperfect or had been trampled. We spent hours collecting leaves in silence. By nightfall we had many more than I had planned to gather. Sitting by the edge of the road, we picked out the loveliest ones and left the rest there in a pile. The evening light shone between the pines and the air was colder than we had expected when we went out—we hadn't intended to stay out so late. We returned to the house quickly to avoid the cold. I carefully placed the leaves between the pages of my María Moliner Dictionary; I had so many, I needed a big book to keep them in. I forgot about them until Melissa came back from her trip two weeks later. It was November and the leaves had all fallen off the trees. Then I remembered the leaves I had placed between the pages of the dictionary. As I took out the first one, which had been red-orange when I picked it up from the path and was now reddish brown, I remembered with cinematic clarity the look of satisfaction on Mayté's face when she found this perfect leaf, without defects or imperfections. Each leaf reminded me of Mayté, though that was not the reason I had picked them up in the first place. I had gathered them so that Melissa would know that I was thinking of her in her absence and that I loved her. But with each new leaf I saw Mayté's hands as she gave it to me, the way the sun glistened on the first strands of gray in her dark hair, the way we rested on the side of the road as we picked the best leaves.

I handed the leaves to Melissa, who was delighted especially that I had remembered something that she loved so much, even though it didn't have the same significance for me. "That is true love," she said. I smiled and kissed her, thinking that each time I saw the leaves I had gathered for Melissa I would think of Mayté. Now the thought of Mayté came to me spontaneously, without effort, without sitting in the same chair in the same spot we had shared, the way I had in the days after our separation.

That incident perturbed my sense of having found the definitive relationship, but my life was still under control. Dreams, fantasies, and memories are uncontrollable and irrepressible. Actions are something else altogether.

On a Friday months later in the spring, Iris and Rodolfo invited us to a café on Houston and Avenue D where they play Cuban music. The place is a bit seedy—or *cutre*, as the Spaniards say—dark and shabby, where Latin musicians and some black Americans go to unwind. Even though Melissa doesn't usually come with me to concerts or readings in Spanish because she doesn't understand the language, she decided to come along. We arrived early in order to get a table, and I was sitting in front of the small stage. When the musicians began to play, the drummer was directly in front of me; he was a tallish man of indefinite race as most of us are, with his hair back in a braid. I never drink, but that night I had two glasses of wine. That must have helped things, and the fact that spring had just begun. The sun was out, the trees smelled fresh, and it had been a very long winter. The man was playing on stage and I, sitting in front and slightly below him, began to observe him: the power of his hands on the drums, the way he kept the beat with the interior muscle of his right thigh. He exuded an energy that drew my eye to him, and I began to be irritated by his presence, his movements, the way he stared straight ahead into empty space. A typical Latin macho, I thought, and I wanted to kick him, but still I couldn't stop staring at him. Then I started to wonder why I felt such anger toward someone who had done me no wrong, who didn't even know I was there. As if in a trance I said to myself that I could sleep with him, and as a matter of fact I very much wanted to sleep with him. The thought made me smile. Would you believe that after they finished playing, he came over to our table, introduced himself, and sat down beside me and invited me out and I said yes? Right there beside Melissa, who was talking to Iris, he very smoothly asked me to come over to his place the following evening at eight. I accepted. That was the first time I had lied to Melissa. I told her I had a work dinner and that I would be late. And late it was, and my ass was sore as well when I came back. I kissed her and lay down on the bed beside her, disconcerted by my own actions.

Ricky, that's the musician's name, lives in an apartment on Tompkins Square Park. He's married, but his wife, a Venezuelan singer, was on tour in South America. He told me he had come over to our table because he was attracted to my eyes. I was surprised. I didn't think he could see me with the bright stage lights shining in his face. He said that he is used to looking out against the light and that I was very close and was looking at him intensely. This was all so strange that I didn't even answer. It didn't matter much. We went to bed almost immediately. There wasn't much romance, more on my account than on his. The truth is I was obsessed with him and could hardly concentrate on my workshops that day, dreaming of the encounter. Contrary to the power he exuded when he was performing, his voice was soft and his gestures contained, but in bed the man who had played the drums the night before returned. Suddenly I was lying faceup and he was kneeling between my legs. He grabbed me under my thighs, lifting me slightly from the bed. I realized that he was attempting to enter me anally, which I hadn't expected. I protested, but he wasn't listening. He was outside of himself, staring into space, just as he had been when he was playing the drums. He's going to rape me, I thought. It was useless to resist, he would do it anyway, and if I struggled, I would be hurt, God knows how much. So I closed my eyes, opened my legs, and relaxed, hurling every insult a woman from the Los Sitios neighborhood of Havana would have come up with in such a situation, all without opening my mouth:

"Fuck you, you bastard motherfucker!

He penetrated me and it felt like my hips were coming apart, and I cursed him from the bottom of my soul, but an instant later, out of nowhere, I felt an overwhelming orgasm come over me, which I tried unsuccessfully to hold back.

I didn't hear from him until a month later, when his wife was again on vacation and he again invited me over. I told him there was no way in hell, that he was an animal.

"That's not what you said when you were coming underneath me."

"It's true, but now you can just go to hell."

Ricky lived on a high floor, and as I went down the elevator on that night, I said to myself that this was a repeat of my experience years earlier with the restaurant cook. My life now was completely different from the one I had with Jerry, but apparently there were still some cracks through which dissatisfaction had seeped in. I spent two months reflecting on my life, and I began calling Mayté more frequently and inviting her to go out for coffee or have sushi, just the two of us. She would accept and we would talk about Raquelita and Ana Gabriela, who were now living on their own, about movies and Cuba— a subject that we more or less agree on—and we complained about the cuts in education spending and the wild increase in the rents in the city—a subject we agree on completely. But we never talked about ourselves. It was as if our past had never existed... until the first day of snow last year. That morning, as I drank my coffee in bed, I said to myself, What if I tell Mayté how much I missed her when she left, how much I cried? What if I tell her about all the ways I devised to keep our rites intact and not forget her, that I've never found a scent that affects me like the one between her legs? What if I just tell her?

I always imagine these moments of fundamental self-discovery to be like rivers that I've come to. Each river is deeper than the last. The first was years ago on that June 24th, the restaurant was the second, my disarray after the end of the relationship with Mayté was the third, and Ricky was the fourth. Daring to tell Mayté that I had almost died when she left me would be the fifth, and number five represents the human soul. Just as humanity is made up of good and evil, five is the first number created by the sum of a pair and an odd number—I read this in one of my esoteric books. We have five senses. Five is the number of love and it is closely associated with the human soul. It is the number of Ochún. My sentimental soliloquy sounded like a melodrama, but I didn't care. The same people who make fun of love kill themselves and each other out of jealousy, just like in Mexican movies from the forties or the radio soaps my mother listened to when I was little. I had been brave to accomplish the things I had in my life, but what if I was able to reveal the innermost core of my heart, that very heart that was in the center of my chest and that ached when I thought about her. If I were able to tell her, if I could actually do it, it would be the bravest act of my life. That confession was my one chance, no matter the outcome, to keep myself from going to bed with strangers who would break my ass in two or fill me with oily *chicharrones* to drive up my cholesterol.

And I did it, without modesty or restraint, just as I'm telling you now. I told her that when she left, my heart was shattered, that my soul bled each time I looked at the corner that we had decorated together, that when I left that house, I thought that my hopes were destroyed forever. And to my surprise she, who was so reticent in her emotions, began to cry, and between the hiccups she also confessed to a whole series of sentimentalities. We made love, and despite the years that had gone by since the last time, her scent was still the best. When we got up, she warned me that she wouldn't leave her apartment, but that if I moved into hers, we could record a message with both of our voices on the answering machine. I told her that I would move into the one above hers, which was empty and which also has five windows on the same side. After all those years I had learned something. Our relationship had a chance only if we were capable of maintaining boundaries.

I announced that I would restart my sexuality workshops. If you want to triumph in life, you have to be in tune with the times and the historical moment you are living in. With all those TV shows where people make money out of their worst failings by telling things about themselves without reserve, even making things up, and having to live in a country where the president's likes and dislikes are dinner conversation, for God's sake, who cares if I like the smell of a woman who hasn't bathed in three days? And you know what? By the way the workshops have been more successful than ever since I began inviting Mayté to come along every once in a while to give her side of the story. It has worked so well that I even invited Ricky to come for a presentation next month. Veronica, his wife, loved the idea and promised to come too, so that the public could get her perspective. Now I know that they have an open relationship, in other words, they sleep with other people, together or on their own. I don't really want to highlight that aspect in my workshops, but I am thinking about bringing the guy who made the *mofongo con chicharrones*, who I hear is married and lives somewhere around Mount Vernon.

Now I really have to go. But before I do, I wanted to ask you something I've wondered about for years. You don't have to answer me right away. Someday, if you feel like it, call me. I know that you and Iris are friends. She is one of the most serene people I know, happy with her husband, daughter, job, and friends. And I know that Rodolfo isn't part of your friendship with her because she has made it clear to me that I shouldn't let him know that you two know each other. How did the two of you meet?

About the Author

Sonia Rivera-Valdés was born in Cuba and first lived in New York City in 1966. Considered one of the most important writers from Cuba, she has had stories appear in many anthologies in the United States, Europe, and Latin America, including *Cubana* (Beacon Press, 1998) and *Dream with No Name: Contemporary Fiction from Cuba* (Seven Stories Press, 1999). She is president of Latino Artists Round Table (LART), a cultural organization established in New York. She has written extensively on Latin American and Hispanic literature, and is a professor of Latin American Literature at York College. Rivera-Valdés won the prestigious Casa de las Américas Literature Award in 1997. She lives in New York.

About the Translators

DICK CLUSTER is a novelist and translator. His other translations of Cuban fiction include the anthology *Cubana: Contemporary Fiction by Cuban Women* and works by Alejandro Hernández Díaz, Antonio José Ponte, and Pedro de Jesús.

Of *The Forbidden Stories*, Dick Cluster translated the explanatory note, "The Scent of Wild Desire," "Between Friends," "Lunacy," "Adela's Beautiful Eyes," and "The Most Forbidden of All."

MARINA HARSS is on staff at *The New Yorker*, and is a translator of both fiction and nonfiction from Spanish, Italian, and French. Her articles and interviews have appeared in *Bomb*. Her translation of Rogelio Saunders Chile appears in the fall 2000 issue of *Autodafe*.

Of *The Forbidden Stories*, Marina Harss translated "The Fifth River."

MARK SCHAFER, a poet and visual artist, has translated the works of novelist Alberto Ruy Sánchez, short story writer Jesús Gardea, and poet Gloria Gervita, among many others. His next projects include translating Béln Gopegui's novel, *La escala de los mapas*, and publishing his translation of Antonio Jose Ponte's book of essays, *Las comidas profundas*. He lives in Boston.

Of *The Forbidden Stories*, Mark Schafer translated "Five Windows on the Same Side" and "Catching On."

ALAN WEST-DÚRAN has written poetry, essays, and children's literature. He has translated the works of Luis Rafael Sanchez and Rosario Ferré, among others. Most recently he translated into the Spanish Cristina Garcia's *The Agüero Sisters* and, into the English, Alejo Carpentier's *La música en Cuba*.

Of *The Forbidden Stories*, Alan West-Dúran translated "Little Poisons."